What the Bird Sees in Flight

Collected Stories of a New Zealand Farming Family

Joseph R. Goodall

Listening Leaves Press

Listening Leaves Press
Atlanta, GA

For more information visit: www.jrgoodall.com.

Paperback ISBN 978-1-7368194-0-1
eBook ISBN 978-1-7368194-1-8

Edited by Elizabeth A. White.
Cover art by Elizabeth Lang.
Cover design and author photo by Becca Goodall.
Typesetting and illustrations by Joseph R. Goodall.
Printed by Lightning Source, LLC.

First paperback edition April 2021.

Dedicated to John Russell Goodall —

I am his namesake and grandson, he is my inspiration as a writer and man.

The Hester Family Tree

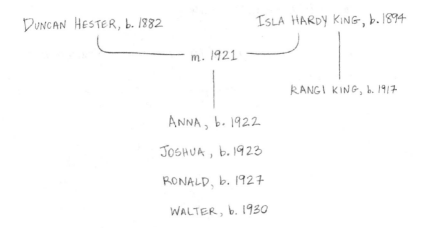

Duncan Hester, b. 1882

Isla Hardy King, b. 1894

m. 1921

Rangi King, b. 1917

Anna, b. 1922

Joshua, b. 1923

Ronald, b. 1927

Walter, b. 1930

NEW ZEALAND

aotearoa

"LAND OF THE LONG
WHITE CLOUD"

Table of Contents

The Farmhouse — Whare Pāmu

The Limping Farmer

Matamata, 1957

"Isla, hand me that bucket will you, love?" Duncan took the bucket from his wife and slopped the pigs. He leaned over, wincing, as the hefty animals swarmed around them.

Isla stood tall, her gum boots sinking in the mud as she held Duncan's arm steady. Her face wrinkled as it twisted into a grimace, yet she was noticeably younger than her husband.

"Careful, dear, you'll topple over right into the muck," she said.

"These pigs are ready." Duncan gave her a quick peck on the cheek as he straightened.

"Didn't you say you wanted to count them?" she asked.

"I did."

"Will you remember the number?"

"Of course, there's less than twenty." Duncan lumbered out of the pigpen, Isla trying to keep up. They walked along the fence line toward their small house, rising and falling across gentle, deep green hills. The fence divided their property in two, extending from the main thoroughfare to a winding stream that fed into the Waikato River. Duncan maintained a brisk pace despite his weak leg and heavy breathing. Isla told him she was worried about his heart, but he continued on, using both the fence posts and his wife's arm for support. Dense clouds filled the sky above them, dark gray and heavy like the pockmarked stones covering the hill behind their house.

"Why won't you get Ron or Wally to come help?" She inspected his face, which was coarse with gray stubble.

Duncan didn't answer.

"Duncan, dear, have you spoken to them lately?" Her voice raised an octave.

Duncan still didn't answer as they neared a gate in the fence. Instead, he pet the snouts of two cows that came to greet them from the other side.

"I think you should call them," Isla said, pressing her luck.

"Ron and Wally?" Duncan searched through the items in his pockets.

"Yes. And the other children." Isla hoped Duncan would understand her train of thought.

"Take a look at ya, old girls." Duncan said to the cows, offering them some feed. Isla pursed her lips and looked the cows over as well.

"Remember when Anna named one of the cows Miss Perkins? She had it in her mind for so long that Miss Perkins was her *horse*." A smile crept across her face.

Duncan nodded, his face still grave. Isla helped him wrap a measuring tape around the cows' bodies. This time, she abstained from asking if he'd remember the numbers.

"Will you really sell all of them?" she asked on their way to the chicken coop.

"What gave you that idea?" Duncan scowled, making eye contact with Isla and betraying a hint of warmth in his gaze.

She eyed him warily. "I saw your notes at the telephone."

"You've been on my case all year." He gestured, looking away. "Figured I'd finally oblige. I've some good offers for the cows and the pigs," he said matter-of-factly, as if he'd kept his wife abreast of his plans from the beginning.

"I told you I can manage. You need to be focused on your health," Isla said as her husband struggled to open each latch of the custom-made chicken coop.

"I won't be here forever. It's my job to sort out the farm business."

"And who said that?"

"I want you to be well cared for," Duncan said.

The constrained birds burst from the cage, cackling and immediately scouring the rich floodplain soil for food. Isla insisted that she feed the chickens after Duncan began struggling with the bag of grain. As the birds pecked at her boots, Isla suddenly burst out laughing.

"What are you carrying on about?" Duncan tossed the half-emptied bag into the nearby shed and fiddled with the keys to lock it.

"Remember when the boys would scare the chickens? Rangi would lead them all in his scare dance. Chooks chooks chooks!" She waddled haphazardly and squealed, sending the frightened chickens scurrying away. Her body shuddered in mirth. She shot a glance toward Duncan, who was looking at his dirty hands.

"I was probably too hard on them, wasn't I?" He kept his head down.

Isla approached him and hooked her arm under his. "You taught them all so much."

"Sometimes I wonder if it accomplished anything." Duncan fixed his eyes forward again. Isla stayed quiet. Any response she could offer felt like forcing water into an overflowing pitcher.

Rain began to fall in large drops as they hobbled back to the farmhouse, arm in arm. Their home was elevated off the ground with large stones and had settled unevenly, giving it a slight, oddly charming lean. A trellis circled the crawl space, wild plants winding through it in every direction. A sparse collection of trees were anchored into the hill behind the house, the land rising into the distance like a wavy green backdrop. It felt like home, but it also felt quiet and sad.

Inside, Isla prepared cups of tea and they sat down at the round, wooden table in the kitchen as part of their morning routine. Duncan was still breathing heavily as he jabbed his chest with his knuckles. Isla watched him, trying to remain calm. When he began to clutch his shirt, just below the collar, she quickly stood and helped him to bed, reassuring him softly. Her words were as much for her comfort as his; her stomach was in knots.

"I need to make a call. I need to tell Jim Brown about the cows and pigs," Duncan said as soon as his head met the pillow.

"No you don't. You need to rest." She placed her hand gently on his chest. She thought he seemed better. They stared at each other as if playing chess.

"I know you're trying to sell the farm," Isla finally said.

"It's time."

"I know. I was hoping you'd come around. It's sad, but we can't take care of it anymore."

"I don't want you to have to care for it on your own."

"Don't you worry about me, Duncan Hester."

Duncan stared across the room, as if viewing a presence invisible to Isla. The light filtering through the window was just bright enough to see that Duncan's eyes were heavy with tears.

"You need to call the children. They have a right to know. It's just as much theirs as ours." Isla felt a sense of urgency.

"I will, in time."

"All of them?" she whispered.

"I'm in a bad way, love. Can we talk later?" He closed his eyes.

"I'm going to call the doctor, just to be safe." Isla patted Duncan's hand, surprised that he did not protest, and retreated to the kitchen.

Nostalgic memories seemed to project onto the room around her like the walls of a maze, like heart-wrenching obstacles on her way to the telephone. A faint ring of dark gray was still burned into the wall above an electrical outlet, marking the spot where Rangi had caused a small fire while building a radio set. From a dusty corner of the sitting room came the echoes of Anna practicing scales, classical music, and hymns where the upright piano had once stood, before it was sold to pay for more feed. Beyond the dining table was a wooden chest where Joshua had stored his carefully-acquired insect collection, the contents of which he'd used to terrorize his siblings and then eventually as fishing bait. The shelves of Isla's fabric and yarn along one wall of the kitchen had originally contained Ron's and Wally's inventions, metal and wood scraps assembled and torn apart and then given new life as yet another contraption.

Finally at the phone, Isla dialed the local doctor, her sense of time still fluid as she rotated each number like turning back the hands of a clock.

After three attempts, the doctor had still not picked up.

She bit her tongue to hold back curses and looked down at the worn desk surface. Duncan's slanted scrawl filled her view, his collection of dates, sums and reminders written on numerous tea-stained pages, his customary organization progressively unraveling. Numbers from that afternoon caught her eye. She blinked and scanned the list again, confirming to her dismay that Duncan had written incorrect quantities for the chickens, cows and pigs they had recently inspected.

Soon she had her brother in law, Gordon, who was also a doctor, on the other line. She worried that she would not be able to hide her ragged breathing.

"His memory will come and go, Isla," Gordon said. "It's good that you're keeping an eye on him."

Gordon had a way of oversimplifying everything, even mental illness. Usually Isla found it grounding, reassuring. Now it was infuriating. She wanted to demand an explanation that he could not give. She wanted more time.

Isla scurried to the shelves by the window overlooking one of the cow pastures, rifled through a box and removed piles of woven yarn. Ten, twenty, thirty pieces completed this month. With a call to her neighbor she could get these to a ladies' group and a shop in the town center and pull in a decent profit. The same woman could get her more supplies at a bargain...

The ideas buzzed through her mind until another piercing cough came from the bedroom, and she shot to her feet like a toy soldier at attention.

Isla tried to slow down, to breathe.

"Take care of yourself," Gordon had said before she hung up without a goodbye. She hadn't mentioned Duncan's chest pain, cough, or persistently ailing leg. The local doctor would have to deal with those. But her husband's memories? Their family? Their home?

The window rattled as a gust of wind came against the house. Outside, the grasses of the field were in motion like the choppy surf off Raglan coast, bowing in alternating directions like a tide. A rainbow of wildflowers blanketed the hillside, waves of purple, yellow and red petals brilliant today but gone tomorrow.

Isla stowed her knitting away and returned to the bed holding a plainly framed picture.

"I know you're an old man and can't see as well as you used to, but I want you to look at their faces again." She handed him the picture and leaned toward him on the bed. Rangi, Anna, Joshua, Ron and Wally stared back at them, frozen in time. Duncan clutched the frame with trembling hands.

"I always like to think Rangi looks like you, too." She ran a finger over the image, pointing to the tallest boy, her firstborn, his dark hair and olive skin a stark contrast to the other family members.

"We've lost him, Isla. You know he doesn't want to stay in touch."

"We must write to him at least. I don't care about the money, I just want them all to know. To be part of it if they want to."

"Listen, we can leave Joshua out of this, too, since he left the country. That's fair." Duncan wheezed.

"You told me you claimed Rangi as your son. You can't ignore him any more." Isla watched her husband's jaw set, his glistening eyes bulge in their sockets, and she immediately regretted her words.

Duncan grunted and forced the picture from her hand, sending it to the wooden floor with a clatter.

"This isn't about Rangi or Joshua, or about any of the children," he said. "They made their intentions known when they left. We have to make ends meet for ourselves, Isla."

Isla peered down at the image of her children, immortalized in their youth, the glass over their faces now fractured. She clasped her hands together as if in prayer and turned back to the bed.

"This is our home, Duncan. Where the children grew up, where we've grown old together. When we release it, I want it to be as a family."

"No one wants the damn farm!" Duncan shouted, before his body erupted into a violent string of coughs.

Isla rubbed her husband's shoulder and kissed his forehead. She waited to respond, hoping he'd concede.

The Fantail — Pīwakawaka

The Boy Who Wouldn't Grow Up

Matamata, 1937

Duncan's legs trembled as he struggled to maintain his footing on the sweltering metal roof. His breathing grew shallow, labored and rapid.

"Mr. Hester, let me take the tin snips." Amrit wiped sweat from the thin line of forehead below his gray turban. He stretched out his arm and grabbed the long-handled tool from Duncan.

"This is tough work for only two people." Duncan rolled over to his back and let his legs relax, his chest heaving under his clasped hands. The heavy cotton covering his body trapped hot air and sweat against his skin, but it was an effective shield from the merciless sun overhead and the scorching corrugated steel under his backside. He let his eyes close and thanked heaven for the sudden breeze rushing over them, ten feet above the ground. The cow shed roof had a mild pitch, perfect for collecting rain during the wetter months. But frequent hail storms and the shoddy workmanship of the farm's previous owner meant the metal roof needed repairing if Duncan was going to be able to collect enough water for all the cows.

"We're nearly there," Duncan said, his breathing back to normal. Amrit did not reply.

Duncan opened his eyes and sat up. Next to him, the brown-skinned man was kneeling over the tin snips as he cut a steel panel to the right size, his mustache quivering like a rabbit's tail. Swiveling his hips with a grunt, Duncan managed to shift his weight to his knees again. He seized a rope to measure the next panel, marking the line for Amrit to cut.

"Amrit, about your brother..."

"Mr. Hester, please accept my apologies." Amrit paused from his work and looked into Duncan's eyes, his chin downturned, his head bobbing ever so slightly from side to side. "My brother is not feeling well today."

"No harm done, it's not your fault. Well, yes, there is some harm done—we won't have completed my to-do list before Isla's family arrives."

Amrit returned to his work without responding. The small man had an excellent work ethic, complemented by being closemouthed and demure. Duncan sometimes wondered if he intimidated Amrit, whom he had hired after the man's family immigrated from northern India. Duncan was a man of few words himself, but he did enjoy learning about Amrit's culture and way of life; the Punjabi man had plenty of farming knowledge from his own country. Duncan was even considering selling a couple dozen acres to Amrit when the man was ready to strike out on his own. But Amrit's brother was another story. Gurson was an inebriate, no doubt trying to find the bottom of a bottle somewhere this morning. Certainly not being of any good use.

Duncan stroked his graying beard and retrieved his notebook from his back pocket. "I'll need your help tomorrow, too, if you're available," he said as he ran his pencil over the list on the wrinkled paper. "We need to pasteurize the next batch for market. And Joshua and Rangi are supposed to be assembling some new storage barrels. Anna will promptly be filling those, with Charlie's help."

"Yes, of course, Mr. Hester," Amrit said.

"Having Sylvia and Gordon this afternoon will slow us down." Duncan eyed the dirt road, which snaked past the house, the horse barn, and through the cow paddocks. He frowned as he made a note to talk about finances with Gordon, his brother-in-law. If he wrote it down, he would do it, despite the burning in his throat.

'I will be sure to bring Gurson tomorrow, to double our efforts," Amrit said.

'If he's better, but I won't count on it." Duncan could not bring himself to be direct, as much as Gurson needed someone to splash a bucket of cold water in his face.

'I'm praying he sees the error of his ways. When he gets hungry he sobers up."

Duncan shook his head as he marked the second cutting edge. 'I've already circulated an advertisement for another helper. I've sold more sheep and am doubling down on the dairy production. If only those South Islanders wouldn't keep flooding the market up here in Waikato. We don't need more farmers, we need better farmers. And sheep farming is just not as profitable as it used to be. If only they'd wake up and smell the roses or, better yet, look at the export rates. But the government dole just makes people lazy and stupid. Those ministers in Wellington are only making everything worse."

Amrit maintained his silence and his steady hand, pinning the fresh metal into place with a hammer. Amrit did not indulge Duncan's political musings. It was when he was particularly heated that Duncan became long-winded, his frustrated thoughts spilling out as inefficacious tirades. In his mind, the American stock market held the world in its sweaty grip and still had them all boiling together in a pot of its greedy making, this Great Depression. But it was no use dwelling on these high-minded, world-away musings. Macroeconomics would not keep his farm running or his sheep, cows and family fed.

Duncan passed the marked sheet metal to Amrit and sat up to stretch his fifty-five-year-old back. Over the ridge of the silver roof, the Kaimai mountains on the horizon were obscured by wispy clouds. In the foreground, herds of black, white, and brown cows grazed undulating hills of sunburned grass, which were drained of their usual deep green. A few flocks of sheep wandered along the fence line, which Duncan's sons Rangi and Joshua were supposed to be repairing.

A squeaking mass of gray and white feathers fluttered past Duncan's face, startling him, nearly sending him off balance. Three fantails alighted on the grooved metal, chattering and pecking, accordion plumes waving on each of their tiny rears. One of the birds bounced up the sloped roof to the ridge, chirping in distress in response to the hot metal under its delicate feet. It turned its beak toward the sky and flapped its wings but failed to lift off again. The other two fantails zoomed forward, whistling loudly as if to scare the apprehensive bird from its perch. The trio leapt together from the roof and haphazardly flew north toward the mountain range.

"Go ask those rain clouds to come over here, why don't you?" Duncan huffed as he returned to the next piece of metal at his knees.

The surrounding farmland, with its spindly fir trees and scarred, stony soil, marshlands with thorny brambles, and hills etched with the concentric paths of grazing sheep, was like an intricate machine, whirring and ticking away under Duncan's careful hand. Not that the land needed him to survive, he conceded. Aotearoa, as the native Maori people called New Zealand, was a paradise alive and breathing all her own. Mankind—Pacific Islander, European, and Asian alike—shared in the effort of stewarding this land, albeit amidst mistrust and infighting. From Duncan's perspective, the people inherited the land as it was left by the previous generation, and they were responsible for the effects of altering it to suit their needs. Relying on the land for survival was tough, global economic crisis or not. But as he etched another mark into the sheet metal, Duncan reminded himself he had chosen this way of life, just as his father had chosen, a decade before Duncan was born, to journey across oceans to this small, green island in the Pacific.

'Dad, won't you tell Joshua to get off his ass and help me?' Rangi's voice stung like a barb in Duncan's ear.

'Rangi, don't take that tone with me.' Duncan gritted his teeth and peered over the edge of the roof. His eldest son, his stepson, stood in the browned grass with his arms folded and his black hair an unruly mess above his offended, raven eyes.

'He's not pulling his weight. I can't repair the fence by myself, for goodness' sake. He's just sitting there, spitting out insults. Can't you talk some sense into him?' Rangi was now gesturing with his arms above his head, his face turned to the sky as if performing a rain dance. This young man, nineteen now, was increasingly willful, argumentative, and irritable. Somehow, the younger son, Joshua, had rubbed off on him.

Duncan sighed heavily. 'I've spent my patience with that boy,' he grumbled.

'I'm trying to finish the job quickly, believe me. I need to fix my radio today before the ham radio net.' Rangi was pacing now, his childlike delight for his amateur radio hobby a bubbling energy he could not contain. 'I can't miss this meeting or they'll boot me from the group.'

'Calm down, Rangi. I'll go speak to him.' Duncan swung his legs over and descended the ladder. 'Now poor Amrit has to work on the roof by himself while we go wrangle your brother.'

'It's OK, sir, I'm making good time.' Amrit tented his fingers in front of his face and bowed before disappearing further up the roof to secure the next panel.

'I needn't say it, but this fence is very important, what with the calves wandering away.' Duncan's chest tightened as he reflected on how much each calf meant to their livelihood. He lit a cigarette as they proceeded north, past the house. The motion calmed him, as much as he hated the habit.

"We had half a dozen posts installed and were anchoring the wires, but then Joshua started ragging on me." Rangi kept his eyes forward and took long strides, staying ahead of Duncan.

"You ought to be able to work this out, being the older brother—" Duncan began.

"He's your son," Rangi said darkly.

Duncan stopped. He felt like he was swallowing his own words. He remembered the day early in their marriage when he had vowed to Isla, her face flush and tear-stained, never to refer to Rangi as her son. He was theirs, as were all their children.

"Hold it," Duncan bellowed, snuffing the cigarette beneath the toe of his boot. "Stop walking."

Rangi turned abruptly, glowering, clouds of dust forming at his planted feet. Duncan took a breath and stepped forward, praying he could see Rangi as his young boy, though that child was nearly impossible to distinguish in the full-grown man looming before him now.

"Rangi, son," Duncan continued in a softer tone. "I know Joshua is difficult. I will deal with him. But that fence needs to be completed before Uncle Gordon arrives."

"Yes, sir." Rangi eyed him suspiciously, then resumed his march toward the gap in the fence.

"Now, about the radio…" Duncan pictured the outdated radio set he had almost sold years back, the one that had brought them news of economic downturn, government inaction and misappropriation, rumors of war and famine. It was Rangi's side project now, despite Duncan's wishes.

"What about it?" Rangi shot back.

'Do you remember our conversation about the furniture pieces? I thought you were trying to finish two of them by the end of the month. It's good money, Rangi."

'I don't like woodworking, Dad. I'm not good at it."

'But I learned from a Maori woodworker. I thought you would benefit from learning."

'I'm not Maori." Rangi's pace slowed as they approached the deteriorated fence.

'Yes, you are. They're your people." Duncan knew better than to specifically mention Rangi's dad.

'I didn't grow up going to a *marae* to learn about Maori culture. I don't know any Maori. I didn't think you respected Maori people." Rangi enunciated each word forcefully, deliberately. 'I don't want to be a Maori."

Duncan was silent as he hung his head. His son knew better than to talk back to him. Rangi had certainly turned a corner, and Duncan was left without a map for navigation.

'Dad, this radio net is important. I've been given a call sign now." Rangi stopped at the gap in the fence but still faced the mountains, his back to Duncan. Joshua was nowhere in sight.

'Does it make any money?"

'I'm doing fine here on the farm. You said I could stay."

'If you started your own income stream. Look at me, Rangi. Do I really need to say it again?"

Rangi's response was muffled by an obnoxious car horn. A jet-black Austin Twelve with a shiny chrome radiator grille rumbled toward them, gleaming in the noonday sun as a cloud of dust and gravel billowed in its wake.

Duncan raised his arm to wave, thankful the grimace on his face was masked by his squinting in the sunlight. Two brown-haired heads emerged from a window, along with small hands waving in return.

"There are your cousins. Go tell your mother her sister has arrived." Duncan began to trudge back toward the dirt road.

"But Joshua—"

"I'll find him. Go tell your mother."

Duncan met up with the car as it stopped near the horse barn. A well-dressed man, woman and two children emerged from wing-like doors on each side of the vehicle. Duncan's daughter, Anna, walked out of the barn with a squeal.

"Hello, how wonderful to see you all." Anna's long, black braid flopped over her shoulder as she bent to kiss her young cousins, Geoffrey and Leah, on the cheek. She was holding a wooden, bristled brush in one hand and a clump of papers in the other.

"Hi, Anna darling," Isla's sister, Sylvia, cooed as she embraced Anna. Despite the heat, Sylvia's wide shoulders were wrapped with a fur coat. A red dress clung to her straight, narrow hips before swelling out around her long, thin legs. Blond hair extended from her close-fitting cloche hat in a tight curl around each ear.

Geoffrey and Leah began to climb on the gates of the horse stalls, giggling. They were gangly like their mother, but their flyaway brown hair resembled their father's.

A rather tense voice approached Duncan from the side. "Good afternoon, Duncan."

"Ah, Gordon. Welcome." Duncan turned and shook his brother-in-law's hand three times and then thumbed his own suspenders.

"Wonderful day, isn't it?" Gordon Campbell's forehead was like the white cathedral cliffs along the Coromandel Peninsula: tall, fissured, and shiny with moisture. He swiped at his receding hairline with a handkerchief, which he promptly returned to his coat pocket before buttoning the front of his gray, tweed, three-piece suit.

"It's a scorcher. Hasn't rained in weeks." Duncan scratched his neck, which was rough with stubble.

"I did say to Sylvia on the way in that it looks rather browner than I'd remembered."

"Gives us more time to get work done."

"Yes, of course." Gordon eyed the land like he owned it, which he did, in part. But not for long, if Duncan could buy back his share. Gordon was a healer of humans, a well-paid physician, while Duncan was barely making ends meet in his over fifteen-year attempt to ameliorate this farmland, which had been ravaged by deforestation and poor soil management.

"Daddy, can I ride the horse?" Leah trilled, scurrying to Gordon and scooping his fingers into her hand.

Gordon chuckled. "Only if Anna says you can."

Good, thought Duncan, he knows his place. The animals belong to the Hesters.

"Later, Leah. I promise," said Anna, approaching them with even more papers in her hands now. "I've just finished grooming them and now I'm preparing for a surprise after dinner. Why don't you and Geoffrey come help me? You can be part of it."

"A surprise?" Sylvia interjected. "What on earth would you be surprising us with?"

"It's a play," Anna said. "Mum read us *Peter Pan* growing up and I just got a copy of the play from a friend. I thought, with Leah and Geoffrey coming, we'd have enough of us to fill all the most important roles. It'll be a bit improvised, of course." She made eye contact with Duncan and winked.

Anna was by far the most creative and playful of his children, and she had a knack for bringing them together with lighthearted

25

activities. Duncan had never been a proponent of imaginative storytelling, as he even found the stories in the Bible hard to believe at times. But he knew his wife would love the idea of this play.

There was a guilty throb in his core as he considered Rangi's love of ham radio. It had always been a perplexing pastime to Duncan, but it consumed his son's attention. The difference was, he told himself, fifteen-year-old Anna had already expressed her desire to be a teacher, which was a fitting and achievable profession that seemed to bring her joy. Any interests she had on the side would be secondary to this pursuit. For Rangi, there was no such passion for a viable occupation. He had long since made it clear he did not want to be a farmer, and now it seemed he'd turned his nose up to woodworking as well.

"A play sounds lovely," Sylvia said, her eyes twinkling.

"Isn't that the production we just saw in Auckland, Syl?" Gordon said.

"Yes, with the boy from Neverland who wouldn't grow up." Sylvia grinned.

"It's rather far-fetched, but the children love it." Gordon cocked his head in a supercilious manner, while Leah, still gripping his fingers, swung his arm in glee.

"Come." Anna extended her hand to the children. "You can join my preparations in the barn. It's cooler in there, too."

"I reckon Geoffrey should lend your sons a hand. He's nearly thirteen," Gordon said over Leah's squeals.

"Dad, really?" Geoffrey slumped his shoulders, looking awfully like a rag doll with his red cheeks and crisp, store-bought shirt and slacks.

"Yes, son, ask your Uncle Duncan what you can do to help."

Duncan frowned slightly, feeling patronized. Geoffrey looked up at him as if he knew exactly what his uncle was thinking.

"We'll head over to the south paddock. Ron and Wally are down there with one of the farmhands spreading cobalt." Duncan tipped his hat to Anna, then thrust his hands into his deep pockets as he set out again.

He led the way to the paddock with Gordon and Geoffrey following behind, while Sylvia tiptoed in her fancy shoes to the house to greet Isla.

"What's cobalt for?" Geoffrey asked.

"The cows and sheep need cobalt for their health. The soil is lacking this material, so we spread cobalt salts for the animals to eat as they graze." The problem was, Duncan had not been able to find an efficient way to spread the salts on their two hundred acres of grazing land. So, they were left to apply the salts by hand, one paddock at a time.

"This will be good for you, Geoffrey, to see how livestock is handled," Gordon shouted as the wind mercifully picked up.

"I've been here before," the boy protested.

"Yes, but you're becoming a man now. And most men work with their hands for a living."

Duncan raised his eyebrows, curious if Gordon was encouraging his son that he could be a farmer, or warning him of the path ahead if he eschewed higher education and life in metropolitan Auckland.

The south paddock was down the slope from the house, consisting of several acres of flat land along the banks of the winding stream that bordered their property. During the wet season, Duncan had to be careful of the cows sinking into the earth here, as it was quickly liquified by rainfall. But today, scores of cows ranged in the idyllic beige expanse, browsing for the last of the edible greenery. Dark-haired Ron and fair-headed Wally, Duncan's two youngest sons, were interspersed among the cows, spreading salts, along with an aging, heavyset farmhand named Charlie.

"I do apologize that we weren't all there to meet you, Gordon." Duncan cupped a hand over his eyes as he tried to survey how much of the paddock was still to be covered.

"Say nothing of it."

"We didn't finish everything I meant to before you arrived."

"For crying out loud, I'm not here as an inspector." Gordon guffawed.

Despite himself, Duncan smirked. He cast down his gaze and pulled out his notebook again, underlining the reminder to talk about purchasing the land back from Gordon and adding a second note to discipline Joshua.

"Ahoy there," Charlie hollered in a Scottish accent as he leaned against a scraggly pine tree and scratched his backside. The balding man had worked with Duncan for over a decade. As they approached the old man, he flashed them a smile of tiny teeth like corn kernels.

"You remember Gordon, Charlie? And this is his son, Geoffrey."

Charlie tipped his bowler hat to the newcomers.

"Geoffrey is going to help you finish out the paddock. Should be able to complete it before sundown."

"I reckon so, with another pair of hands," Charlie said good-naturedly, although he viewed Geoffrey's clean clothes warily.

"Hello, Geoffrey." Ron trotted over, an empty bucket slung over his shoulder. He was tall for a ten-year-old as far as Duncan was concerned, since he was nearly as tall as his older cousin. A beat later, Wally joined them as well, hunching over to catch his breath. His grin was still missing some teeth, seeing as he was only seven years old.

"Daddy, we came up with a new way to spread the salts," Wally announced.

"Is that so?" Duncan ruffled his son's hair and gave him a pat on the back.

"It's still in the works," Ron added.

"But it will make this all go faster." Wally put his hands on his hips. "We'll add slots to the bottoms of a couple old wheelbarrows, and Charlie will add a rotor that spits out the salts in each direction as you push the barrow forward."

"It's worth a try," Charlie said.

"Yes, I could see that. Good thinking, lads." Duncan nodded with a smile. He stroked the back of a cow grazing past them. "Why don't you show your cousin how this is done? I need to talk business with your uncle before dinnertime." Duncan swallowed and checked Gordon's reaction out of the corner of his eye. The man was stone-faced and heavily perspiring.

"And then we'll perform our play." Wally skipped forward and jumped over a bucket, landing with a thud on his gum-booted feet.

"Wally, it's a surprise," Ron scolded.

Wally frowned. "Just for Mum. Dad won't care about it."

Duncan chuckled, though feeling not a little hurt. "Anna told me. I'm looking forward to seeing it."

"What sort of business did we need to discuss?" Gordon asked on their way back up the hill. He tugged at his collar and wiped sweat from his face yet again.

"Well, I figured with you being in Auckland you might have a better sense of the state of things, of the market, of the outlook ahead." Duncan's words were as cryptic as his thoughts as he tried to determine how best to make his proposition. His wife would be the first to accuse him of perennially beating around the bush.

"I'm not a fortune-teller, if that's what you're asking." Gordon's beady eyes roved as if searching for a shelter from the sun. "But personally, I believe we're on the up-and-up. With farm debts being subsidized by the government, and new state-sponsored agricultural research being conducted, things are looking more hopeful."

Duncan's hands reflexively fisted. "As good as that is for some, I'm more concerned about farmers moving past what's been done and reading the signs. Being smart with their resources and making the most of what they have, rather than just surviving on handouts."

"That's precisely what the research is for," Gordon continued tenuously.

"No, I disagree. If parliament would do what they were meant to and represent us, instead of handing down from on high what they think is best—"

"I don't think we will get far in this discussion, Duncan," Gordon said in a haughty tone.

Duncan swore under his breath, angry at himself more than at his brother-in-law. He was nowhere closer to getting his plan across.

"You're probably right," he muttered.

They were approaching the cow shed. Amrit's silhouette was at the top of the ramshackle structure that Duncan had deferred on renovating when he first purchased the property outright in the early Twenties—before he'd been forced to seek out Gordon's assistance rather than leaning on the government's crutch.

"Was there something else you meant to bring up?" Gordon rested his shoulder against the side of the shed and retrieved a cigarette from his pocket, which he lit. Duncan waved his hand to refuse a smoke when Gordon offered. He had to stay focused.

"As a matter of fact, yes. There's no need to respond to this request now, but I've been thinking about our agreement—"

Duncan was interrupted by a thunderous sneeze from inside the shed. He ducked inside the doorway and grabbed hold of his son Joshua's collar, yanking his body out into the harsh afternoon light.

"Ouch, Dad, watch it," the freckled, towheaded thirteen-year-old whined, dragging his heels in the dirt as he brushed straw from his shirt and pants.

"Be careful, young man," Duncan warned. "If your uncle wasn't standing here, I would tan your hide."

"Duncan, what is going on?" Gordon asked, his cigarette bobbing on his lips.

"I have no idea," Joshua whimpered.

The metal roof rattled and pinged as Amrit scuttled to observe the goings-on. The fantails were back as well, cooing and chirping as they preened on the edge of the roof.

"Joshua, you know damn well what you did. You left your brother alone and failed to see your task through to completion. What do you have to say for yourself?" Duncan's arms quivered in anger. It seemed everything at the farm was spiraling out of his control, and just when he was trying to demonstrate he was taking steps forward.

"Rangi was going on and on about his radio. I was really the one working, if you're interested in my side of the story." Joshua's eyes drooped pathetically; he was a master at playing the victim.

"And why were you hiding in the shed just now?" Duncan yelled, his neck bulging, his patience on a razor's edge.

Joshua hemmed and hawed, unable to string two words together.

"Mr. Hester, if I may," Amrit said from above. "Joshua came to borrow a hammer after you left. I told him you were looking for him."

"Right," Joshua yelped, regaining his speech. "And then Rangi showed up and we got in a row. Look what he did to me!" He pointed to his eye, which Duncan suddenly noticed was puffy and red, bruising slightly.

"I told him I would take care of it," Duncan said.

"Mr. Hester, I tried to make peace," Amrit said in almost a moan.

"Did you see who started it?"

"I...I don't know," the Indian man admitted.

A bell rang out, vibrating the air around them.

"That will be the call for tea." Gordon extinguished his cigarette butt with his toe and set out for the house at a swift pace.

Amrit scurried down the ladder and looked down at Joshua, then up at Duncan pleadingly. Joshua stood gingerly, groaning as he rubbed his eye. He blinked with a wince and then ran off after his uncle.

"I'm sorry, Amrit, I shouldn't have brought you into this." Duncan looked at the man who had loyally worked for him nearly three years. The destructive path of Duncan's wrath was like a vacuum, mercilessly taking in things and people, to his great regret. He stepped back and surveyed the roof, which was now completed. "Excellent work, that will do nicely."

"Very good, sir." Amrit's head wobbled back and forth in agreement.

"Come eat with us. Isla wouldn't hear otherwise."

They descended on the house in a pack: Duncan, Amrit, Joshua and Gordon from the cow shed; Anna and Leah from the horse barn; and the boys and Charlie from the south paddock. Isla and Sylvia were inside, singing Psalms from the Bible open on the counter as their curly blond hair shone, graced by the sun's descending rays. Isla was a homespun, yet warmer version of her sister. Her hair was held behind her head in a simple bun, and she wore a stained, white apron over a faded blue dress. Her face, manifesting exuberance and determination as she sang and retrieved plates from a cabinet, was just beginning to wrinkle around her eyes and mouth, though of course Duncan would never mention this to her.

The dense hardwood dining table was laden with an array of colorful foods for afternoon tea. Isla maneuvered around the handcrafted table delivering platters, plates, cutlery and fresh flowers, her head swiveling like a watchful hen as she dished out orders to each of the children, all the while wearing a contented grin. It was a great improvement over her anxious state of the last several days. Hosting guests was a great joy to her, but the recent hardscrabble years had put her out of practice, and she had been stressing over the state of the house, their clothes, and the lack of fancy recipes.

But one look at the spread of dishes on the table and Duncan's mouth watered. Aromatic roasted lamb with mint sauce, sliced beetroot with peas and carrots, boiled potatoes dressed with green herbs, and freshly prepared butter alongside loaves of bread, which Sylvia had picked up from a local bakery. The children vied for a spot around the table, their eyes wide with hunger, their mouths stretched in merry anticipation. Isla's worry had been needless.

Duncan grasped his wife by the shoulders and kissed her neck.

'Hello, love. Everything OK?' Her eyes betrayed concern as she took in Duncan's demeanor.

'It will be,' he said.

'Come in, Amrit, come in. Is your brother here, too?' Isla continued her frenzied preparations.

'No, madam.' Amrit bowed respectfully.

'Gordon, welcome.' Isla paused to kiss her brother-in-law on the cheek, who remained stoic and merely nodded in return.

'I think everyone's here.' Sylvia surveyed the faces around the table. 'Oh, Geoffrey.' She clucked her tongue at her son, whose face was smudged, his clothes disheveled and stained.

'Dad wanted me to be a man,' Geoffrey said. Ron, standing at his side, gave him a clap on the back. Gordon chuckled as his wife glared at him.

'Where's Rangi?' Isla asked, removing her apron. Only then did Duncan notice his absence.

'I spoke with him earlier.' Duncan peered out of the largest window in the main room of the house. Three bedrooms branched off of this room. Their only toilet was an outhouse around the rear. Outside, the hills were bare, the animals having retreated to the shed or the clusters of trees along the stream. There was no sign of Rangi.

'Joshua! What happened to you?" Isla cried.

'It's nothing, Mum." Joshua shooed her away.

'Duncan, come bless the food so we can start, then you can go and track him down." Isla beckoned him with her free hand. Everyone else in the room formed an oval of linked hands around the table. Gordon and Charlie removed their hats. Duncan kept his on; a fair concession, he reasoned, as Amrit's head was always wrapped in his turban.

As he prayed aloud, Duncan's mind descended into a fog. By the time everyone had served their plates and began to tuck into their food, his thoughts were on Rangi, the rest of the room a haze to his senses. Try as he may, he was transfixed at the table, unable to go outside, unsure of how far Rangi might have run and how difficult it would be to talk to his grown, yet unmotivated son.

Joshua was noticeably quiet during their meal, as he was usually the most talkative and boisterous at the table. Duncan, on the other hand, was usually taciturn, letting Isla lead the dinnertime conversation, particularly when guests were present. No one seemed to notice he was deep in thought, mulling over the great web of expectation he had devised over his family and his farm.

'Will everyone join us out at the horse barn? We have a surprise to show you," Anna announced after clearing the table. 'Mum, you too. We'll clean the dishes for you later," she added, making sure to catch her mother's attention before Isla could retreat to the kitchen.

'My, my, what is this about?" Isla asked innocently.

'Come on, it will do you good." Sylvia grabbed her sister's elbow. "Take my coat," she said, slinging her golden fur over Isla's shoulders.

"The sun will be going down soon, after all." Isla giggled as she walked out the door, making eye contact with Duncan.

"You too, Dad," Wally said, pushing Duncan forward in the small of his back.

Leah ushered her dad from the table, and Ron led Charlie and Geoffrey outside. The sky was cast in hues of violet and apricot, and long clouds stretched toward them from the mountain peaks, promising rain. The fantails followed them overhead, flitting up and down in their irregular flight, without a care for economics or professions or growing up.

As the group ambled up the slope to the barn, Duncan found Joshua at his elbow.

"Do you know where Rangi is, Joshua?" Duncan asked quietly, as calmly as he could.

Joshua pointed ahead of them with a disinterested expression. Sure enough, Rangi stood tall at the main door to the horse barn, crowned with an elaborate pirate's hat and a hook strapped to one wrist. At his side there was a stool, upon which sat his prized radio with its crosshatch, round speaker, its antenna extended toward the sky.

"Aye, mateys," Rangi growled. "Gather 'round for a story that'll tickle yer ears and warm yer hearts."

"Thank you, Rangi—I mean, Captain Hook." Anna laughed. "Come, come, there are seats set up already." She shepherded the adults to a semicircle of mismatched chairs, a bench, and stools.

Amrit profusely congratulated Anna, before the play had even begun, while Charlie led Isla to the premier seat and Sylvia gushed to her husband about the props and stage pieces Anna had created. Joshua mischievously pounced for the feather in Rangi's hat, at which Rangi extended his wooden sword and directed his younger brother to walk the plank. Beaming with pride, Rangi looked back to the audience and caught his father's gaze.

In that moment, Duncan couldn't decipher how Rangi felt toward him, his son's eyes gleeful yet mysterious as he settled into this unexpected and dastardly acting role. As Duncan sat next to his wife, who took his hand and smiled at him, he realized how little he knew his children as they were, rather than how he envisaged them.

The fog lifted from Duncan's consciousness as the boys and girls donned their costumes and arranged themselves on the makeshift stage in front of the horse barn. As Rangi switched on his radio and turned the dial to a precise position, orchestral music filtered into the evening air and led them on toward Neverland.

The Boy Who Wouldn't Grow Up

The Sailboat — Waka Tere

The Whales Beneath

Tory Channel, 1956

The small fishing boat tacked east and west, making its way south along the Tory Channel toward Picton. The two men aboard were broad shouldered, with knit caps over their long, dark hair. Rocks jutted upward sharply from the sea to starboard. Beyond them, the land formed a backdrop of brown wrinkles. To port, narrow peninsulas extended out toward the boat, forming small, shallow bays where ships liked to run aground. It was getting late in the day, and they still hadn't caught anything.

Mikaere cracked open a beer and took a swig. From his perch on the other side of the mast, Rangi tried to imagine what the drink would feel like going down his throat, which was currently salty from the ocean spray. He tried to remember why he'd agreed to help his friend with his far-fetched scheme to bring in a haul of mackerel. Rangi had spent much less time on the ocean than Mikaere. He was a land dweller, a farmer's runaway son, and his upset stomach was the only reason he didn't join the other man drinking. Seasickness was almost akin to intoxication—light-headedness, distorted vision, and vomit—but without any of the more pleasant, albeit temporary, side effects.

"They hated her." Mikaere pulled a net into the boat as he spoke, the Maori tattoo patterns wrapped around his forearms rippling. "The first time I bring a woman home for them to meet and they hate her."

Rangi, barely listening, kept noticing instead where Mikaere left his bottle, instinctively positioning himself to catch it if the boat shifted unexpectedly. Why didn't his friend pay more attention to his things?

'Do you even know what I'm talking about?" Mikaere adjusted the sail to increase their speed. 'You've dated a *Pakeha* before, I'm sure. What gets me is this girl really could be the one. I wouldn't have taken her to meet my parents otherwise, white girl or not. My mum doesn't know about all the women I've been with. She wouldn't want to. But this one is special."

'I haven't dared take a girl home, even now that my parents are practically on their deathbed." Rangi felt awkward just sitting on a crate, but he truly couldn't bring himself to stand up.

'Of course you haven't. You never go home." Mikaere laughed deeply from his belly.

Rangi took a deep breath. The wind was on his back, so he hoped Mikaere couldn't hear his curses.

'I'm telling it like it is, ain't I?" Mikaere shouted over the wind.

'Leave me be," Rangi said.

'Damn, you're terrible at conversation."

Rangi finally stood and leaned over the side of the boat. Gigantic mammals circled beneath the choppy surf. A jet of warm mist shot into the air as a whale surfaced nearby. He'd never seen a whale so close before.

'Pull your own weight, won't you?" Mikaere threw him a rope to coil. He had brought the boat to a standstill and was gathering a net to cast.

"There are some humpbacks below us," Rangi said, struggling to wrap the rope around his arm, still distracted by creatures.

Mikaere inspected the turquoise water, which sparkled like the underside of a *paua* shell. 'What such strange beasts. Takes a hell of an operation to bring 'em in," he said, his neck craned over the bow. "My mate was on one of the last ships to hunt those things. You know they say the entire industry's over."

Rangi nodded, continuing to wind the rope over, under.

"Have you ever been on a whaling ship?" Mikaere asked, throwing the net out into the water with a labored grunt.

"I used to work on the docks," Rangi croaked, pausing to rub his abdomen.

"Yes, of course. You told me that. You were the only Islander, weren't you?"

"I'm used to it."

"What's it like? I mean, your mum's a *Pakeha*, isn't she?" Mikaere gave him a genuinely curious look.

Rangi spread his feet further apart and closed his eyes. His body felt like rubber. He wasn't sure if it was shame, withdrawal, or the seasickness.

"Hurl over the side, mate, or you'll be scrubbing the decks." Mikaere seemed to finally take notice of his condition.

"I'm OK." Rangi opened his eyes and looked at another whale surfacing, deciding to tell more of his story. "Yes, my mum's white. My dad was Maori, but he was killed during the first War."

"So you're an old bastard then?"

"I'll be forty next year."

Mikaere chuckled. "No, I mean your dad knocked up your—"

"They were married." Rangi tossed the coiled rope into a pile on the deck.

"Oh, wow. That doesn't happen." Mikaere surveyed the horizon as he prepared another net.

"Well, they were. But my mom remarried later. A businessman more than ten years older than her, who then started a dairy farm. I was just a little tyke, but then all of a sudden I had four younger siblings. It was a blur."

"I think that's the most you've ever told me about yourself."

Rangi staggered to the side and vomited. Now his mouth was sour, but at least the churning in his stomach subsided.

"I didn't mean to make you sick." Mikaere tossed his empty bottle in a canvas bag and then reached for a new one.

"Throw me one, will you?" Rangi said, his hands on his knees, staring into the grimy, tan deck.

"You sure? I know how you get," Mikaere said condescendingly.

"I need it."

"Yeah, just not too much. We need to catch something if we're gonna make this trip worthwhile."

"You're drinking."

"Not like you do." Mikaere tossed Rangi a cold bottle.

Rangi threw his head back and felt the chilled rush of beer through his chest. He didn't notice the taste—it was a light, flavorless brew—but he was immediately at ease to be drinking.

"You don't think it's bad, do you?" Mikaere asked.

"What?" Rangi licked the foam off his lips.

"Me being with a white woman."

"Hell, no. I thought you were asking about the beer. It's terrible."

Mikaere mockingly stepped back in shock. "You feeling better now?"

"Yeah, I'm fine," Rangi said, but his gut was disagreeing with him again. Still, he continued chugging his beer.

"Well, how's it like for you? Is it easier to date a white lady or a Maori?"

The question Rangi hadn't wanted to think about or answer. "Shit, it's just the color of her skin."

'I don't see you with many women." Mikaere checked the nets stretched over the side.

Rangi cursed at his friend, cast his emptied bottle over the railing, and wobbled angrily toward the stern. He ran his fingers through his thinning hair and clenched his other hand tightly into a fist. It was a while before he realized he'd been staring cross-eyed at the same rock, lost in thought about jumping overboard to join his bottle.

'Come here, mate! Help me haul this in." The urgency in Mikaere's voice convinced Rangi to take him seriously. He was surprised to find the other man straining to bring a net onboard. Once they'd heaved the load of fish onto the deck, both men sat back against the side of the boat, breathing heavily.

'Do you know about *kaitiaki*?" Mikaere asked.

'Is that the Maori name for these fish?"

'No, mate, it's the name given to whale guides. *Kaitiaki* led the canoes of our ancestors to this land."

"I don't know why I'm missing my sea legs then," Rangi quipped.

"Listen, I know it really bothers you that you didn't grow up in a Maori family. But you're not alone, eh? We all find our way in our own time, with the right direction. What's it gonna take? If Tangaroa, the god of the sea, rose from this water himself and claimed you as his son, would you consider yourself Maori?"

Rangi stared blankly out toward the horizon, his thoughts pulled back to his childhood.

"There was one time where my mum set me up with this white girl in our church," he said in halting speech, as if talking to himself. 'Honestly, we hit it off. I didn't think we would. Then a while later, when we were walking through town, she made these snide comments about a Maori family, and then another about a group of Islander men at a bar. It was then I knew she didn't really see me. I was just one of her people."

'What did you do?" Mikaere asked quietly, reminding Rangi he wasn't alone.

"That was around the time I left town. I never saw her again."

'She was a bush girl, probably never left her own town. City women like some brown skin." Mikaere growled lasciviously. Rangi feigned a half smile. They sat silently for a minute. Memories continued to rush through Rangi's mind. He felt less sick as he talked openly, so he eventually continued.

'I fell in love with a Maori woman on the coast a few years back. She had the most lovely hair and eyes, and a keen sense of business. She was a chief's daughter, the whole lot. But you wouldn't have known from the way she carried herself. She worked on the dock because she wanted to. And she had a connection with animals, like me."

'Don't worry, I won't make a joke about your connection with animals." Mikaere tugged at the net to keep the fish contained.

Rangi glared at Mikaere.

'She sounds like a keeper," Mikaere said, straight-faced.

'She was wild, carefree, brilliant. I wanted to spend the rest of my life with her."

'Did her father not take a liking to you?"

'I never met him. I couldn't. I don't know anything about Maori tradition. It gnawed at me. I don't think she saw me as one of her people. I was just the bloke at the dock she had a thing for. I picked up and left soon after."

As the sun set, the boat rocked and the dying fish in the net flopped at their feet.

'Well, if my woman and I have a kid, I'll be sure you're the godfather."

'You've thought ahead about that?"

'I just did." Mikaere laughed.

For some reason, those words meant something to Rangi. Mikaere reached over and squeezed his friend's shoulder. Rangi was suddenly conscious that he was leaning back against Mikaere's other arm. He thought about when he and his brothers used to pile into the tiny cow shed on their farm to hide away from their dad's chores, their bodies huddled close as they took turns peeking through the small window, surfacing carefully like the whales beneath the boat coming up for air. He turned his head to look at his friend.

"Thanks, mate."

Mikaere smirked. "You want another?" He stood and retrieved two more beers.

"No, I couldn't stomach it."

Rangi hoped he could stay sober when they got back to land.

The Book — Pukapuka

Praying for the Family

Jagged shadows rippled across the ceiling above Anna's head. When she squinted, the rough blotches of plaster attempting to hide long settling cracks looked instead like an abandoned field of carelessly tilled rows.

Anna lowered her gaze to the patterned rug on which she sat, rotating her shoulders and flexing her legs to restore circulation. She couldn't get her imagination to slow down, even though her body had been still for most of three hours. The neighbors' monotone chatter sounded like an ancient language through the thin walls, as if from a world away. She had never met them, but it was her only reminder she was not alone. Leaning over and spreading her fingers out over the thick, multi-colored strands woven into the rug, she sighed deeply, feeling like she was hiking through a bog. Praying was not for the faint of heart.

Anna scolded herself. She had it easy, after all. She was used to long, hot days in the African sun. On this dreary day, she hadn't even left her small flat in Auckland's City Center, and it was already afternoon. Laziness was a lot easier to blame for her restlessness than the inundating sense of loneliness in her chest. She pushed her hair, which she hadn't touched since waking up, out of her eyes and braided it absentmindedly behind her back. A new bout of regret hit her for not having returned her mother's call. The pages of the open Bible next to her rustled as her cat, Freckles, nuzzled against her hip.

'OK, boy. I'll give it a few more minutes. Now that you're here with me." Anna rubbed the place on Freckles's head behind his ears that made him melt into a pile at her side. With a deep breath, she clasped her hands together again and leaned on the bed in front of her. She thought about what she'd just been trying to read, the parable of the persistent widow. *I'm neither of those things*, she reasoned. *But I am a stubborn single woman. I guess that's close enough.*

There were so many things producing anxiety in her that she couldn't focus on just one. She had scrawled names and ideas onto a notebook page in front of her, but her curled script grew hazy the longer she stared at it.

The room was filled with boxes she'd never unpacked after her return from overseas. Scores of books stacked to precarious heights on each side of the door, next to her bed as a makeshift table, and under the narrow window looking out on a red-brick alleyway. One book, light brown with silver lettering, sat on the windowsill. Anna's mind wandered to the old woman, Nyawira, her head covered with thin fabric and arms lined with brass hoops, who had given her the book on Anna's last day as a missionary in the Kenya colony. The small Kikuyu woman stood barefoot on her plot of land, gathering the many children she cared for in her strong arms, and looked at Anna with wide, generous eyes.

"Thank you for helping me protect this land, for teaching my children." Anna could vividly remember Nyawira's tears. Certainly some of them were contained in this book, which had belonged to her late husband. It had been a holy moment. Indicative of the many wonderful people she met and served. God was much easier to talk to then.

Anna had been the foreigner, the white woman, but in time became welcomed in many places. Her visceral sense of duty toward her community and the children she taught gave her a daily dose of motivation. Over the years, she became aware of the plight of many local Kikuyu landowners, particularly the widows, and had worked with her missionary society to advocate for them. Of course there had been a lot of other tensions—the political upheaval in Kenya, the cultural differences and misunderstanding, the weeks of debilitating sickness, the devastating betrayal by her school headmistress, and the heartbreaking letters from her mother lamenting the fracturing of their family. But at present, Anna conveniently overlooked those. Or, maybe she was just seeking to adopt a healthier perspective. She hoped so.

Freckles pounced on a wisp of dust as the wind slipped through the cracked window and rustled the well-worn pages of Scripture still open in front of her. The words were like a letter written to a former version of herself. Anna stood, shook her head, and beckoned Freckles out to the kitchen, where she fed him. The counters and living area were in a similar state of disarray as the bedroom. A table with one chair next to a small, circular window held papers, folders and a stash of red pens she used to grade students' assignments. Trying to get her secondary students to understand the real-world importance of literature and writing was like trying to keep at bay all of the questions about her previous life overseas—near impossible. The other teachers, while trying to take a breather in their dingy teachers' break room, would laugh off her concerns. They thought she was paranoid, too high-strung, and not open-minded enough. She wanted to tell them what it was like to see infants die of dehydration or women walking miles for dirty water to drink, but she chose not to.

As Anna cleaned Freckles's bowl, the pile of envelopes on the floor next to the front door caught her eye. She immediately recognized her mum's handwriting on one of the small ones. She opened the bills and junk mail first, leaving the handwritten letter from her parents' farm for last. The torn envelope was rough on her fingers, which began trembling as she held the lined stationary. As she read, her mind was whisked back to the family farm—overfilled milk buckets cutting into her hands, dirt caught in her fingernails, sunrises over green hills, rough sacks of grain and feed. All these memories threatened to be erased by the news that her parents were going to give up their land.

Her knees buckled before she reached the end of the letter, and Freckles scampered off as she took his spot on the carpet. Now, the prayers came easily. Why hadn't her mother called sooner? The room spun and she closed her eyes. She immediately began to devise travel plans to visit her parents in Matamata until, in a moment of clarity, she snatched up the letter and read the last paragraph.

Her parents had already sold the farm. It was too late.

Without hesitation, Anna donned a sweater, grabbed her handbag and left the flat. She walked briskly to the hardware store, as fast as she did down the hallways at school, much faster than she did in Kenya through the village, purposefully avoiding eye contact with passersby. At the store, she bought some soil and seeds and tools. It felt so mechanical, like watching caged animals in the zoo. She had never paid money for soil before.

The woman at the cash register seemed withdrawn and distant. Anna felt so useless just standing there, and she longed to strike up a conversation with the employee. Her mind wandered to the women making food in the wooded hills of East Africa. Always using their hands, never idle. She thought about walking together to worship at the thatched-roof chapel at the top of the hill overlooking the glassy lake. She could hear the ladies' endless chatter while she tried to catch on to the rhythms of communicating in Swahili, wishing it was as easy as joining an ocean current. Eventually, she gained fluency. Even still, she stood out in the village with her fair skin, glossy, straight hair and light brown eyes, but at least she began to understand and be understood.

Now, as Anna faced the young woman in the hardware store, she found herself unable to form words in her native tongue to begin a conversation. What would she talk about? Anna was startled by a sharp voice demanding her attention. The cashier pulled hair out of her eyes and glared at Anna, repeating her request for payment. Handing over the cash, Anna neglected to say thank you as she hurriedly left the store in embarrassment.

When she arrived back at her flat, she went directly to the small patio off the kitchen and focused her attention on a bare patch of ground against the cinder block facade. First, she mixed the store-bought soil with some of the earth next to the crumbling patio concrete. She used her hands without reservation, working the mixture with her fingers in swift, efficient motions. Freckles eyed her through the sliding glass door, as confused by her sudden change in habit as she was.

As Anna added lime fertilizer to the soil, she thought of her dad's hands placed on hers, guiding her, showing her the way. Yet as she lined the garden patch with stones, the sense of nostalgia became supplanted by regret again. The gray stones were like the block walls of the school where she'd taught in Kenya. The headmistress of the school, a British woman as rigid as a statue, had left a letter on the door of Anna's hut, essentially forcing her to resign, to leave the country. Behind the veiled threats in the letter were years of complicity with efforts to take land from local families. Now the school and community would have new leadership, would comply with political and military pressure. Anna's efforts to aid people like Nyawira would no longer be tolerated.

Anna stopped and looked at her progress. The freshly rotated ground in the rectangular plot was loose and airy, a mixture of natural and man-made, local and transplant. A thought crossed her mind—she was as far away from Kenya as she could be, but she still felt like she needed more space, more distance from her past. She pulled the packets of seeds from her pocket and tried desperately to pray again. Her prayers were the seeds and tears she let fall into the tilled soil.

The sun was setting when the man next door came out on the patio next to her. Immediately, she felt her back tense up. As much as she wanted human connection, her neighbor was not her preference. She had seen him in passing only a handful of times during the last few months, but had never talked to him other than exchanging greetings. He was swarthy, mostly bald, with a hooked nose and a gut that hung over his belt through his unbuttoned shirt.

"My wife had a little garden like that." He lit a cigarette between his lips. "She tried to start one almost every year, but it never lasted."

"I didn't know you were married." Of course she didn't. She didn't know anything about his personal life, but she hadn't seen a woman living in the unit next door.

"Not anymore." He tucked his hands into his pockets and rocked from his heels to toes.

Now that Anna thought of it, she had only seen another older man at the apartment next door. His friend, brother, lover? Again, she couldn't think of any other words. He spoke first.

"You learning the neighborhood OK?"

"Yes, it's fine. I used to live in Auckland about ten years ago." Why had she said that? She didn't feel like telling her story, not now. She was busy.

"Where'd you move from?" He sat down on a rusting chair next to his unruly clothesline. Anna feared she'd already lost control of the conversation.

"Well, believe it or not, from Kenya, in Africa." She couldn't bring herself to lie, but she did steal a glance at his reaction.

"I bet that's a story. You missed home too much, eh?" His voice piqued with interest.

Something about his simple question made Anna begin to cry. She stopped trying to forget about the letter, still sitting on the kitchen floor inside her flat. What were her parents doing right now? An ache for her childhood swelled in her chest.

The man sat up in his chair and put out his cigarette. "I'm sorry if I pressed too hard." He wore an expression of true concern.

"Would you look at me, making a fool of myself." Anna wiped her hands on her skirt and then caught her tears with the sleeve of her sweater.

"Why don't we start over? I'm Pete." He gave Anna a small wave.

Anna returned an introduction, still wiping her eyes. She smiled at her neighbor.

"I hope you don't mind me asking, but would you like to come over..." Pete's voice trailed off.

"For tea?" Anna stood up suddenly, her head spinning even though it felt the clearest it had all day. This possibility of genuine connection grew like a fresh hope within her, freeing her from the distractions she'd been clinging to—mindlessly grading papers, unpacking and staring aimlessly out the windows of her flat.

"It's actually both me and my partner," Pete said shyly.

"Yes, I would love to join you for tea." Anna tore the apron over her head then set the packets of seeds next to the planter. They could wait until tomorrow, after she'd called her mum.

"Excellent. Look, you're already halfway over here." Pete grinned.

The Lantern — Rama

Ghost Stories in the Musterers' Hut

Matamata, 1933

Darkness seeped through the corrugated metal walls of the musterers' hut, threatening to overwhelm the lantern sitting on the cold stone floor between Joshua and his friend Ivan. Tomorrow was Joshua's tenth birthday, and he was much too old to be frightened of the night. He tried not to think of the bush outside, its towering trees and spiny branches barricading them from his family's well-lit Waikato farmhouse down the hill. It didn't help his overactive imagination that Ivan was talking about the old lady next door who had recently been found dead in her nightgown on her front porch.

"Johnny said her eyes were starting to rot. Like black beetles in her head." Ivan squinted and scrunched his shoulders against his neck.

"She was ancient. My mum said she died of old age." Joshua glanced nervously around the hut, trying to wipe from his mind the image of Mrs. Glocken's dead face staring at him. The reflective bare walls and shadowy corners provided many places for haunting forms to appear. The rough wooden door, crooked on its hinges, was held shut by a heap of rocks they'd wedged against it. Animal skins covered the far wall of the hut, stretched in odd, patchwork shapes and shriveled at the edges.

"No, she was poisoned." Ivan's bright red hair glowed around the top of his full, round face as he moved closer to the lantern light.

"Poisoned? By a robber?" Joshua whispered.

"By her crazy daughter who wanted her land!" Ivan reached out and grasped Joshua's shoulder for effect, sending a shiver down Joshua's spine.

The lantern flickered violently. Joshua pushed Ivan out of the way so he could hover his hand next to it, willing the flame to continue burning. His dad had said they'd have enough fuel for the whole night if they needed it. Joshua certainly didn't want to go back and let them know he was afraid and needed more light. He shook his head and looked at his friend, who was shivering slightly.

"You're overreacting, Ivan. My mum's tried to talk to Mrs. Glocken before. She was real quiet and never had anyone visit her. I don't reckon she had any children."

"She was bleeding from her mouth. She was poisoned!" Ivan clutched his throat with his hands.

"How do you know?" Joshua's voice was louder now that he was more skeptical. He really did want his friend to like him, but sometimes Ivan got carried away.

"Cause her ghost is still around here," Ivan insisted, jamming a finger into his palm. "Everyone knows your ghost only stays around when you've been murdered. Or if you have a message." He waved his hands around in small circles.

"That's silly." Joshua began to wonder if Ivan just wanted to be afraid for the fun of it, or if he was truly bothered by this woman's death. Joshua hadn't given it much thought until now. "But what do you think her message would be, if she had one?" He stared unblinkingly at Ivan, his thoughts succumbing to the eerie idea of old Mrs. Glocken whispering in his ear. For a moment, the hut was silent.

This may be your last night alive.

The spooky voice wafted through the walls of the hut. The boys whipped their heads around but were unable to identify the direction of its source. Joshua snatched up the lantern handle, causing the rays of light to scatter around the room, as his heart beat wildly against his chest.

Suddenly, the wooden door swung open, toppling over the pile of rocks the two boys had stacked against it. A beam of light blinded them.

"Please don't hurt us!" Joshua yelled, closing his eyes tightly.

"We didn't do it," Ivan moaned.

"Oh, knock it off, you two. I ain't the ghost of that old bat," the intruder said.

Joshua lowered the lantern and saw a tall, lanky boy waving a battery-powered torch around the room.

"Bloody hell, Rangi." Joshua jumped to his feet at the sight of his fifteen-year-old half brother, carelessly dropping the lantern to the floor with a clatter.

"Better not let mum catch you swearing like that." Rangi flung his bag onto the ground and tossed his torch on top of it. "You should have seen your faces!"

Joshua glowered, swallowing back the angry words trying to get out of him. At his side, Ivan stood speechless with his arms folded, his forehead and cheeks still pale.

"I thought we said you weren't wanted here!" Joshua stamped his foot against the floor.

"Well, Mum and Dad said I could be. So, Happy Birthday!" Rangi brushed back his jet-black hair and kicked off his boots. He sat down on top of his bag and leaned back against the wall. In the low lighting, his swarthy Maori complexion appeared even darker.

"You're lying," Joshua hissed through his teeth.

"Look, you two can't last out here all night by yourselves."

"Shut up, Rangi. Why don't you go sleep out in the bush? That's what bush people do, ain't it?" Ivan spat.

"Don't get smart with me, Baker. Joshua wouldn't have had the idea to camp out at the hut if I hadn't done it before. Besides, he's afraid already. I can see it." Rangi nestled his head back into his hands, his elbows above him on either side like oversized devil horns.

Joshua hated that Rangi brought up his fifteenth birthday campout. Rangi had begged their mum to let him spend the night at the musterers' hut at the back of their farmland with some of his schoolmates. It had taken a while, but finally their mum and Joshua's dad agreed, although Joshua hadn't been allowed to go. At least not until now that it was his tenth birthday.

"I'm not afraid," Joshua said in a monotone voice, wishing he could be more convincing. He had been so certain tonight would prove how grown-up he was.

"Why'd you have all those rocks against the door then?" Rangi taunted.

"We were just being careful," Ivan said.

"Hey, I've got an idea." Rangi sat up, looking amused. "Let's keep telling ghost stories, but about this hut. And then if you're still here tomorrow morning we'll know you're brave enough." His eyes narrowed. "What d'you say?" He stood up and strode toward them.

Joshua and Ivan instinctively stepped back, further into the darkness away from the lantern.

"I'll take that as a yes, since you've already filled the place with hot air." Rangi unbuttoned and removed his shirt. In just an undershirt, his narrow frame was accentuated by his angular shadow on the wall behind him. He flashed them a haughty grin. Joshua was startled by Ivan clearing his throat.

"You go first." Ivan took a step closer to Rangi, causing the older boy to chuckle and puff out his chest. Ivan was a full foot shorter than Rangi but was stocky, with chubby arms and a much larger shadow. Instead of anger, Joshua now felt worried. He didn't think he could come up with a good ghost story, but he knew Rangi could and that made him nervous.

Rangi waved Ivan off with a laugh. "Fine with me. Why don't we all sit down?"

"I'm good where I am," Joshua said. Ivan nodded in agreement.

"Great. Then we'll all hear your knees knocking." Rangi wore a serious expression, with his upper lip tucked under his lower. Joshua recognized the gleam in his brother's eyes, as if Rangi were planning a mischievous prank at church camp or had found a way to get Joshua in trouble for not doing his farm chores.

Joshua conceded and sat down, and Ivan followed suit, but thankfully Rangi did not react.

"A long time ago this land wasn't a farm, it was a burial ground," Rangi began in a slow and suspenseful storytelling voice. He paced back and forth, his shadow rippling along the metal wall.

"Is this gonna be like a Maori grandma myth or something?" Ivan turned his head sideways and smirked. "I don't think that'll scare me."

Rangi seemed to falter for a moment, but then he continued.

"Every new moon, the Maori chief in this area would gather the families of the recently deceased on this hill. They would cry and wail and then bury their dead family members with animal furs and elaborate clothing. Years later, when the Maori's land was taken from them, this farm was built by European settlers. This hut was where the field workers mustered. They stayed here in the planting and harvesting seasons and then moved on when the work was done. But the Europeans didn't know they'd put the hut up on the grave of the Maori chief's daughter, right at the top of the hill."

"Let me guess, her ghost was there?" Ivan said.

Joshua shushed his friend, much to Rangi's glee. The older boy waved his shirt over the lantern, causing the hut to go almost completely dark for an instant. The two younger boys gasped.

"It was when the new moon came, when the night was at its darkest, that the vengeful ghost was awakened. The ground heaved when the farmhands put out their campfire. They went inside and shut the door tightly, thinking it was just a tremor or some hyperactive moles. But they heard groaning in the bush all night and couldn't sleep. That's when the pelts they'd hung on the walls started to move."

Joshua's eyes shot to the old animal skins currently adorning the hut's wall. Surely the tail on one of them hadn't just twitched? His mind was playing tricks on him. His eyes returned to Rangi, who seemed confident he had their attention.

"The farmhands gathered with their backs in a circle in the dark hut and suddenly found that the floating ghosts of animal stalked toward them, mangy clumps of fur stuck to their rattling bones like moss on rotten tree branches. The wall where the pelts had hung lifeless was now empty. With a rush of wind, the door flew open. The chief's daughter stood there, her wool coat hovering over the ground, her body transparent and glowing. She cursed the men for stealing her land and harming her fellow creatures." Rangi looked around, blinking, and then swung his arm to point to the animal skins on the far wall. "The ghosts of the animals pounced and devoured the farmhands, one by one, and then the chief's daughter sank back into the ground with a bone-chilling cackle."

"Oh, come on. Ghosts can't eat people." Ivan giggled nervously. "Where did you get all that from?"

Rangi sighed and stared at the two younger boys for a moment. "We read about burials in a book at school. And my stepdad told me about the farmhands who used to stay in this hut." Rangi shrugged, resigned to the fact he hadn't scared them. "I've got an even spookier one next."

Joshua thought Rangi had set up a frightening scene, but he agreed the ending was a bit far-fetched. Still, he'd begun to glance at the animal skins on the far wall more often, and had entertained the option of moving the lantern closer to them out of caution.

"Let me think of one now." Ivan straightened the hem of his shirt and stared up at the ceiling.

"No, it's my turn," Joshua said. "You already told the story about Mrs. Glocken."

"That didn't count!" Ivan faced Joshua with a look of disgust.

Joshua opened his eyes wide and pointed back and forth between the two of them in an attempt to remind Ivan they were on the same team.

"Fine," Ivan huffed. "But I go next."

They turned and found that Rangi had sat down on his bag again and was looking very relaxed.

Joshua was having great trouble thinking of a ghost story. He'd been trying all night to keep scary images from popping into his mind, but now he had to let them come freely. His chest began to tighten. He thought about praying the Lord's Prayer, or the Psalm about the Shepherd, which always comforted him, but he couldn't remember the words.

Suddenly, the lantern fluttered out with a startling pop. The two younger boys squealed into the darkness. A moment later, a white light filled the hut, illuminating Rangi's face, which looked a little less relaxed now.

"You nitwit. You're lucky I brought my torch. Did you not bring enough fuel for the lantern?"

"I don't know. I brought what Dad gave me," Joshua said in a shaky voice. "I...I think we better go back to the farmhouse."

"Don't be silly, we're in the middle of our stories," Ivan said, although his voice wavered, too.

"Come on, Joshua, what would your dad think?" Rangi said.

"He's your dad, too."

"No, he's not," Rangi shot back, sounding bitter.

An idea came to Joshua suddenly. One that didn't involve shriveled faces or vengeful Maori chiefs and animal pelts. He thought of the tiny picture of their mum on the mantel in the farmhouse, the one of her standing next to Rangi's dad in a soldier's uniform, both of them with serious faces and looking barely older than children themselves. Joshua had never met Rangi's dad, and neither had Rangi. What if his ghost was nearby? Joshua looked at Rangi's smug expression and wanted desperately to rid him of it. But it seemed too cruel.

Ivan tugged at Joshua's shirt sleeve. "Joshua, if you can't think of one, let me go." They'd both inched closer to Rangi's torch, which had been angled up against a wall, its light cascading outward against the wavy metal.

"I don't think he wants to stay. Said so himself." Rangi inspected his fingernails.

Joshua gave his brother a nasty glare. There was silence in the hut. From down the hill, they heard the wind sweep through the trees. When they heard a low moan, they looked at each other. When the noise came again, it was closer and sounded even more like someone crying in pain.

"I think I feel her, Joshua. I think she's coming for us—Mrs. Glocken," Ivan whispered.

Joshua took a sharp breath at the sound of leaves rustling on the other side of the wall. To Joshua's surprise, Rangi also looked panicked. He grabbed his torch and shone it at Joshua.

"What's that at your feet?" Rangi pointed at the floor.

Joshua felt a tickling sensation on the skin of his leg, and his body tensed. Rangi moved toward him and smacked his hand against Joshua's shoe. A shiny black beetle scurried out from under his leg, trying to return to the darkness. Before Joshua could react, a high-pitched ringing filled the air. It came in sharp bursts, like a menacing laugh.

"That's her!" Ivan cried in terror.

Rangi clamped his hand over Ivan's mouth, who then began to whimper.

"There's something out there," Joshua rasped. He took hold of his brother's arm, and the three of them stood as one against this new presence. It moved closer to the musterers' hut, disturbing leaves in its wake. The trio jumped in fright when a scratch came at the door.

Joshua regretted even thinking about bringing up Rangi's dad. Why hadn't he just invited Rangi to the campout in the first place? Then their stupid ghost stories never would have summoned this monster.

The scratching continued, followed by small, frustrated breaths.

In an instant, Joshua's head cleared just enough for one rational thought to occur to him. "Wait, can't ghosts go through walls?"

Ivan's sniveling subsided. "Yeah. I think you're right."

Rangi moved forward and put his ear to the door. "Who's there?" he called in a voice deeper than his own.

An exasperated bark rang out in response.

Joshua shouldered past Rangi and threw open the door. A dog, wearing a bell on its collar, forced its way into the hut, barreling over Joshua and barking excessively as it zig-zagged across the floor. It had thick, pigeon-toed legs, wet, auburn fur matted against its muscly body, and a great, drooling tongue hanging over its toothy jaw.

With a springing leap, the mongrel pounced against Ivan's chest, who screeched like a tui bird as he fell backward, his red hair flopping over his face. Joshua scrambled to his feet and grabbed the animal around the torso, prying it off his friend. The dog twisted and nipped at Joshua's fingers as Ivan struggled to pick himself up, his limbs trembling as he wore a disgusted expression. The two boys stood shoulder to shoulder, facing the slobbering intruder.

"Rangi, if you come at him from the other side, maybe we can..." The torch's light grew dim again, and Joshua spun around to see Rangi retreating out of the hut's crooked door.

The dog barked again and scurried away in pursuit. Joshua followed, a reluctant Ivan in tow.

Outside, moonlight filtered through the fir tree branches, casting an eerie cross-hatched pattern over the slope above the musterers' hut. Ivan had his hands on Joshua's back as if using him as a shield. A shrill whistle came from beyond a cluster of trees, in the direction of Mrs. Glocken's neighboring farm. The dog's ears perked and its heavy breathing stilled.

"What is it, Rangi?" Joshua asked, no longer nervous about the dog but rather afraid of what he could not see.

Rangi swept the light across the ground, but it failed to penetrate very far into the woods. He kept one arm out to fend off the dog, which began to jump up against his leg.

"Sounds like someone coming," he whispered.

When the whistle came again, Rangi dropped his torch in the dirt and ducked behind a tractor tire leaning against the wall of the hut. Ivan rushed to join him, but Rangi shoved the boy to the ground, causing the dog to begin pawing frantically at Ivan and making the entire forest aware of their position. Joshua ignored the commotion as he crouched down and squinted, trying to detect any movement among the trees. The wind picked up, yanking at the tree branches and carrying the acidic smell of sardines and coffee.

The third whistle coincided with the emergence of a shape from the milky shadows. The bulky form lumbered down the hill toward the boys like an old tree trunk. The domed outline of a head and wide, slumped shoulders came into focus, which appeared to have no neck, arms or legs below it. There was no ethereal glow, no transparent apparition, but Joshua was being approached by the closest thing to a ghost he'd ever seen in his life.

"What have you found, Heck?" the silhouette said in a gravelly voice. It sounded like a woman's.

With a whimper, the dog scampered toward the newcomer. Joshua snatched up the torch and directed it at the figure, who was now less than a stone's throw away.

"Don't come any closer," he warned.

"I have a torch, too, you little ankle-biter. Would you like me to shine it in your eyes? Shut it off. It's a full moon for Christ's sake," the voice said as its shape stepped into the light.

It was a very much solid body, wrapped in an oversized green coat, with only black rubber boots visible below the hem. An arm stretched out from the coat and pet the panting dog. A bright red bandana covered the top of the head, below which an elongated face bore a forehead so prominent, its eyes were obscured by shadows. It took Joshua a moment to register that the new presence appeared to be an old woman greeting her dog.

"Who are you?" Joshua asked, his imagination succumbing to reality.

"You go first, seeing as you're trespassing on my property," the woman said.

"This is our dad's land."

"And who would your dad be?"

"Duncan Hester."

'I've heard the name. But you lot don't look like brothers." She took a few more steps down the hill and the dog followed suit.

'I'm Joshua, this is my brother Rangi, and my friend Ivan. We're camping out here for my birthday." He tried to hold his legs still as he spoke.

The woman took another step, the light finally illuminating her eyes. Her cold, mistrusting stare made Joshua swallow hard. She reached into her coat for an object. A weapon? Instead it was a torch of her own. With a click, the silver and rusty-red side of the hut was covered in light.

'I was never clear on where our land ended. But I do remember coming down this hill as a girl, seeing this hut and climbing the rocks at the bottom of the slope."

The boys were all quiet, dumbstruck.

'Mrs. Glocken?" Joshua asked with a stammer, his skin turning clammy even in the warm night air.

'I'm her daughter, you twit," the woman said, a faint glimmer of a smile on her face. 'I'm not that old. I've been living on my mum's property since she died. You can call me Bez. And this is Heck. Hound from Heck, I call him. He must have heard you buggers making noise, because he ran like an arrow down this hill while we were on our midnight rounds."

'This place is haunted, you know." Ivan stood and craned his head to look around as if another form might approach them at any moment.

'Haunted? Probably only by the ghosts of mum's husbands. They each hoped to outlive her, the bastards. Actually, I reckon she's around herself, just to spite them."

'Have you seen a ghost here?" Joshua asked with renewed skepticism about Bez, reminded of the stories of vengeful ghosts.

The woman seemed to ignore the question. "You're brave to be out here, no doubt. Are you the oldest?"

"No," said Joshua. "My brother—"

"I am," Rangi called as he emerged from behind the tire.

"I thought I saw someone back there. You ought to be more protective as the oldest," said Bez, her heavy eyebrows arching.

"I had my eye on the situation," Rangi said. "Had to be out here with these two since they're so afraid of the dark."

Joshua crossed his arms and forced an angry breath through his nose.

Bez cackled. "Being brave isn't about not being afraid. It's about who has your back. I was an only child growing up, so I've always had a dog to keep me company. Don't go anywhere without him." She gave Heck a pat on the head and lowered the torch down at her side, again plunging her eyes into darkness.

Joshua knew it wasn't his place to question Bez, but the horrid idea of this woman doing her own mother in was stuck in his head like a boot in the mud.

"What happened to your mum?" he asked.

"She passed a few weeks ago. A doctor rung me as her next of kin. We weren't quite on speaking terms."

"So you hadn't been to see her in a while?" Joshua didn't hold back the suspicion in his voice.

"Ah, so you're taking the approach of the other nosy neighbors." Bez was pacing now. Was she getting restless, trying to make a getaway? "You think I bumped her off myself? You've got some pluck for a young lad."

"Shut up, Joshua," Rangi turned and yelled at his younger brother. Ivan whimpered the same admonition from Joshua's side. Heck's startling yaps echoed among the trees.

"Don't bother him. He's got guts," Bez said over her dog's barks. "Don't know how I can convince you, but she brought it upon herself. She was seventy-six and smoked too many damn cigarettes. The place was littered with them when I arrived. I wish I would have tried harder to get through to her."

When Joshua caught sight of Bez's eyes again, their black pupils were large, heavy, sad. He felt himself shrinking, as if his meager ten years were no longer enough to stand up to this woman, to her dead mother, to the mysterious darkness hanging around him or the expansive, wild world beyond.

"Well, now you know this is our property. Keep your dog out of it," Rangi said in a way that would have certainly elicited correction from their father.

"And you lot will have to get used to me as your neighbor. You best look out for the others, young man. And mind your manners to the ghosts." Bez took Heck by the collar and directed him up the hill.

The trio watched the odd pair struggle up the slope until their silhouettes had disappeared over the crest.

"I'm going back home," Rangi said, retreating to the hut to collect his things.

"I thought you said we weren't brave?" Ivan called after him.

Rangi turned and gave him a glare that made the shorter boy cower.

"I think I'll leave, too, Joshua," Ivan muttered as Rangi disappeared.

A panic of abandonment gripped Joshua's chest. "Won't you stay?"

Ivan bit his lip. "No more ghost stories, OK?"

"You too, Rangi?" Joshua asked.

Rangi poked his head around the door frame, his drooping eyes holding a hint of curiosity.

'Look, it's officially my birthday." Joshua pointed to the sky, a gradient of deep purple now visible through the openings in the treetops, a greater level of detail becoming clear in the forest around them.

Without another word, Joshua marched back into the hut and unrolled his mat, surrendering to the fatigue he had been avoiding all night. He sensed the other two boys following him, their bodies soon in a row on the dusty hut floor, drifting to sleep as the morning awoke outside.

The Wood Carving — Whakairo

Sawdust and Bloodstains

A cloud of sawdust hung in the air. Duncan Hester coughed at the particles bristling in his throat as he brushed off his canvas apron, inadvertently releasing more dust into his face. A splinter wedged under his fingernail caused his hand to throb in pain. The gloves in his pocket would have protected his hands but also hindered his connection with the wood, preventing him from feeling the smallest of grooves and ruts in its intricate texture. At this moment, however, he had little to show for his eager craftsmanship.

He delivered a swift kick to the leg of his workbench and clenched his hands into fists. The cherry-colored piece of wood in front of him was misshapen and warped. The angular etched lines were supposed to be curves, and the wrinkled forms were supposed to be the outlines of humans. He snatched up his cup of tea and nursed it, ignoring the wood shavings floating on the surface. It was all the chisel's fault. He turned the tool over in his free hand and thought of how it had betrayed him, skipping around, slipping from his grip, exerting its own will.

Duncan's anger subsided as he emerged from his makeshift woodshop, a shed behind the flat he rented from Ms. Ellen on the outskirts of Hastings. He flicked the pencil from behind his ear and scanned over the items on the to-do list in his leather-bound journal. One by one, he heaved crates of cooking utensils, cast iron pans and crisp white aprons up the hill to the cart in front of the cinder block residence.

"Sorry to make you work on a Sunday, girl," Duncan said to Ginger as he patted the soft, red hair above the horse's muzzle. He took inventory of the items in the cart and waved at a neighbor on his way into the town center, hoping he had not noticed Duncan's absence at church that morning.

Duncan prided himself in his work. He had built himself up since leaving his parents' home in Hamilton at a young age. Staying near the North Island's coasts, he had tried his hand at fishing, whaling, animal husbandry, home building and various types of craftsmanship. Sometimes he wondered if it was just luck that he fell among the right people, like the old man Rimu, who were willing to take him on and give him work to do. It may have been good fortune at first, but after a decade of roaming, Duncan shifted his focus to working for himself. He took his toolbox of skills wherever he went, and with a keen eye determined the needs of the community and quietly and deftly met them.

After another ten years, his supply ordering and delivery business was the backbone of every shop owner in Hastings. He had mastered the art of using his nondescript demeanor and features to his advantage. His efficient work brought results that made his business partners happy, and his restrained speech and stiff mannerisms allowed him to avoid unnecessary conversation. He was recognized all over town, but not well-known, and that was how he liked it.

Ginger nuzzled into his shoulder and sneezed, at which Duncan grabbed her mane and shook playfully. He stuffed the journal into the back of his pants and strode back around the flat, down the vibrant, grassy slope overlooking farmland to the south. Creative energy pulled him back to the shed like a magnet. As important as his deliveries were, the unfinished *kauri* wood taunted him. The grueling workweek he had just endured and the one waiting ahead perched on each of his shoulders to add their own insults. He yanked the stool from beneath the workbench and slumped onto it in a cloud of sawdust.

"You're focusing too much on the tiny specks, the whiny child details." Duncan could hear Rimu in his head. "You must think about the whole, not all the tiny parts. Think of what the bird sees in flight, gliding over the treetops."

The old Maori bloke had taught him the trade of wood carving—the qualities of a wood's grain, strength, colors and textures, and the art of wielding adzes, chisels, saws and carving knives to form the fibrous material. Rimu was a master of *whakairo*, the traditional Maori woodworking style. Duncan met him years ago in the corner of his warehouse, where Rimu practiced the craft as a hobby. Rimu's pieces ranged from artistic carvings to furniture and tools, each with a creative and unique style that eschewed the bland products of a modern factory.

Ever the learner, Duncan spent his spare time observing Rimu's work when he wasn't organizing his clients' inventory. Rimu was skeptical of Duncan's proposition of turning his hobby into a business, and Duncan was wary of Maori culture then, worried he would catch a spirit from the wood of an ancient *waka* warship or elicit the ire of a Maori ancestor against his European blood. However, Rimu was graciously kind, if not naively trusting, and the industrious craftsman agreed to a business deal. With Duncan's help, demand for his work grew exponentially over the next few years. One day, however, Rimu held up his hand and told Duncan he was finished with the business.

"I've lost my way, Duncan. I can't speak through my work anymore. I'm only thinking of the money, not the tradition or the art. I can't feel it like I used to."

At the time, Duncan had protested, and because of his disappointment soon lost touch with Rimu, who took his woodworking back to the corner of the warehouse. Now, Duncan understood the old man's dissatisfaction. On top of his daily shipping and delivery duties and client meetings, he had made his own woodworking shop and pretended he had gained some of Rimu's skill. The butchered piece of kauri wood, recovered from a shipment from Auckland, was his latest attempt to get the web of thoughts from his mind out into the world, to make sense of his direction in life and the fears that gnawed at him. But he was a tree grub boring into the wood rather than a bird soaring overhead; fresh vision eluded him.

"Yoo-hoo, Duncan!" Ms. Ellen popped her head over the clothesline at the back patio and waved. "You have another call from the train station." She liked to pretend she was his secretary, although he did not pay her for it.

He swiped at the sweaty hair plastered to his forehead and walked up to the kitchen to take the call. The train station attendant notified him another shipment had arrived for Mr. Dawes's butcher shop on Main Street. His heart fluttered as he thought of the woman behind the counter there, Isla, and her blonde, curly hair, bright smile and lovely round eyes. He felt the urge to be close to her, to hold her.

He asked the attendant if the train from Matamata was on time, and she confirmed it was still scheduled to arrive in three hours. His mind raced as he replaced the telephone on the table.

"Will you be seeing that exquisite young woman again today?" Ms. Ellen appeared at the door with a smile and fresh cup of tea. She had restrained herself for years from pestering Duncan about his love life, but the last few weeks she had delivered a barrage of questions about the clerk at Mr. Dawes's shop. As usual, he pretended she hadn't asked.

'I have a number of errands to attend to this afternoon. If I get another call, please just take a message." He took the cup of tea from his landlady and left the kitchen.

Duncan continued to think of Isla as he returned to the shed, how quickly she caught onto his brooding persona, his biting wit and persistent curiosity. She was a well of deep thought, bravery and compassion. He thought of her hands, slender yet strong, soft and graceful, moving rapidly to perform messy tasks at the butcher. He wondered if she noticed how closely he watched her work, mesmerized by her confidence and skill, or if she continued undeterred, all the while knowing she was under his gaze. Back at his workbench, Duncan donned the gloves this time, picturing Isla's fingers interlocking with his as they walked in the park during their last evening together.

She had spoken of losing her parents in an accident a year ago. At a scenic stop, she pulled his hand to her face and looked him directly in the eyes. Time slowed down as she haltingly told him of her late husband, who was killed overseas in the Great War, and her young son, who lived in a nearby town with her sister. She swayed back and forth as she expounded on her experience. Duncan grew dizzy, willing himself to stand firm though overwhelmed by the new information.

After all the loss she had faced, Isla said she diagnosed herself with a broken heart and decided to take a year off from being a mum. As cruel as it sounded, she had a hard time taking care of herself, much less having a child to tend to. Upon disembarking from the train in Hastings, she took a job at the butcher shop and blindly stepped into a new life.

She braved sordid rumors whispered about her and coworkers resistant to her presence and became a favorite of the customers who frequented the shop. Duncan had seen this firsthand. When he was hired by Mr. Dawes to expand his network of meat suppliers, he was taken aback by how quickly he was drawn to Isla's vivaciousness. He was so out of touch with courtship and romance he waited weeks to talk to her directly. She spoke first, asking intelligent questions of his plans to improve Mr. Dawes's business. His chest was immediately taut, like a sail under the influence of a strong wind. Blessedly, Isla seemed to sense his awe and patiently conversed with him, and Duncan left with the impression she was interested in him as well.

On their walk in the park, Isla's confession of her shattered family brought him to the brink of his own fractured reality. Teary-eyed, he was speechless when she asked for a response. Instead, she pursed her lips and then rested her head on his shoulder as they sat under a tree.

The piece of kauri at his gloved fingertips was still mostly rectangular, with reddish brown grains rippling in waves across the ragged etchings he'd attempted to carve. He thought of his father, Isla's father, and the father of Isla's son, all absent, though their forms and legacies lived on in the children they'd produced.

With a grunt, he secured the wood to the workbench and shaved off layers from its surface with a plane. He could still see the simple outline of the deepest of his previous cuttings, but decided to let them remain. He took a knife and free-formed the outline of a curlicue, like new growth on a silver fern. He thought of the distance between Isla and himself, the uncertainty, the passion, the fear, and the possibility of partnering together. He thought of the distance between Isla and her son, her dead husband and parents. Duncan thought of his loneliness despite the wealth of business opportunities he'd forged for himself. Over the noise of his fear, he sensed a longing for this son whom Isla was running from. He stepped back for a moment, squeezed his eyes shut and remembered old Rimu's instruction. Focus filtered in like light through foliage. He bent over the wood again and, with care, traced the outline of a face, shoulders, arm and then another face, without pausing to second-guess himself. A third form appeared between the two faces and the bridged arm as he continued to carve.

Maybe he was looking for a family.

Maybe this was his opportunity.

~ ~ ~

Isla King's white apron was splotched with red. She avoided breathing through her nose while separating out the clumps of excess pig fat to be used for lard. Setting down the bloody chef's knife, she surveyed the butchered pig splayed on the table before her with satisfaction.

Isla had purposefully waited to don the apron and gloves until after her coworker Biff had gone down the street for more packing paper and string. The men she worked with were always uncomfortable with her wielding a knife. Mr. Dawes Sr., the first owner of the butcher shop, had taught her all about preparing each cut of meat during the war, before her son was born. After Isla returned to work at the shop a few years later, Dawes Sr. had retired, leaving the business to his son and a new generation of butchers who were much less welcoming to her. Interesting peacetime tactic, she thought.

There was a jingle from beyond the checkout counter and her chest tightened. She hurriedly wrapped the pork cuts, removed her gloves and tucked unruly sandy blonde ringlets back into her hairnet. It was unusual for Biff to return through the front, but maybe she had locked the back door out of habit. Besides, there were never any customers on a Sunday afternoon. She left the apron on, as she saw no reason to hide the fact she'd been working, and walked out to the front.

"Biff, I meant nothing disrespectful to your work. I was simply bored to tears." She stopped short when she saw the newcomer from the back, his jet-black hair and gray tweed suit immediately recognizable. The man swiveled around at the sound of her voice. His face creased around his eyes and mouth as he grinned widely.

"Isla, you look lovely." Duncan strode forward with deliberate steps and stopped just in front of the counter.

"Duncan, what a surprise. I...I didn't know you were coming today. Mr. Dawes isn't in."

"The shipment was a day early. I figured I'd come by and drop it off now. I left it out back. No need to bother him."

Isla gasped, remembering the apron around her neck. "Bollocks, I'm covered in blood." She tore the apron over her head, the hairnet popping off as well. "I wasn't ready for this."

"I'm sorry to come without warning." Duncan hunched his shoulders and pulled a leather journal from his coat, which he bent nervously.

"No, no, don't worry about it. I'm glad to see you." Isla took a deep breath. She felt the familiar tug of her lungs fighting to leave her chest. She crouched and retrieved the hairnet.

"I have some other business to attend to in town. I can come back later. However, I was hoping you'd come with me. I've something to show you." Duncan smiled weakly.

"Yes, of course, I would love to." Isla wondered if he wanted to go back to the park. If he had anything else to say about their last conversation. She sighed as she remembered Biff. "But I'm waiting for my coworker to come back. He left the store with me."

"Is that the man passed out in front? He was snoring rather loudly on my way in."

"Good heavens! On a Sunday? How did he manage that?" She rushed around the counter and looked out the window, rather conscious she hadn't made physical contact with Duncan yet. She sensed him stepping closer to her.

"What a mess. He'll have plenty to do when he wakes. I think we'll just have to close up shop early." She turned back to Duncan with a smirk.

Hidden beneath his heavy eyebrows, Duncan's eyes met hers. For a fleeting moment, Isla thought about taking Duncan into the back room and kissing his pleasant face. Then she remembered the blood on her hands. She chided herself for thinking too quickly; it was a heart-racing thought, but it certainly wasn't appropriate.

"Should I wake the fellow outside?" Duncan asked, checking the watch in his pocket.

"That would be wonderful. Would you mind bringing him in? I'll just be a minute." Isla threw her apron in a wicker basket behind the counter, then stomped her foot. The brass-rimmed wall clock told her she'd been working far longer than expected.

"Damn it, I'm late!" She wiped her hands and arms on a towel, grabbed her purse and tidied the hair pinned together on the top of her head. She spun around in a mad dash toward the door and collided with Biff, whose arm was wrapped around Duncan's neck.

"No need to be in such a rush," he said, supporting Isla's unconscious coworker around his back.

"Put him over here, please." She directed him to a chair and then hovered around, wringing her hands. How could she have forgotten? Duncan's spell was too strong. "Duncan, I'm so sorry, but something's come up. I won't be able to join you." She nodded once and then walked to the front door without looking back.

"Isla, hold on. What's the matter?" Duncan's voice was even but coursed with genuine concern.

Isla breathed deeply. She heard Biff moan as he began to stir. The stench of alcohol on his breath overpowered the scent of the carcasses wafting in from the warehouse.

"I was so hoping you'd join me in town. I have a few errands." Duncan ignored Biff's groggy attempts to get his attention. He swiftly strode to Isla, grasping at her hand.

Duncan's unexpected appearance and pleading began to bother Isla. Why had he come today? Of course he wouldn't have known she was to pick her son up from her sister at the train station. But her surprise and embarrassment quickly morphed into annoyance. After their last conversation, he didn't seem ready to meet her son. And she didn't owe him an explanation.

"Hey, what are you lot doing in h-here? W-we're closed. It's S-Sunday aftern-noon." Biff's knees buckled as he tried to stagger along, clutching to the countertop.

"Don't worry, Biff. We're leaving." Isla pushed through the front door and slipped from Duncan's grasp.

"Isla! Isla, please wait." Duncan flew through the door in pursuit, a few steps behind Isla's path across the cobblestone street outside the butcher's storefront.

The sun was low on the horizon, partially hidden by the wooden buildings on their right. The cool, damp air seemed to carry the smell of the ocean even from a mile away. Once on the other side of the street, Isla folded her arms and gripped at the arms of her coat. A man on a ladder paused at his attempt to light a street lamp to tip his hat at them. Isla formed a strained smile in return. Duncan stood in front of her again. She took in the intensity in his eyes, the smell of his coat, his freshly shaven face.

Isla sighed, unwilling to hold back any longer. "I have to go to the train station."

"Why? I just came from there."

"To meet my sister and pick up my son."

"Right. I've been wanting to meet him," Duncan said without hesitation, at which Isla's heart rate quickened. She furrowed her brow, but he didn't seem to notice. "The northbound train was delayed, so we have some time before they arrive. I need to stop by another store on the way. Do you mind if we go there first? And then there's a man I'm supposed to meet at the town square."

Isla turned her face away in feigned resignation. "OK." Inside, she was elated to spend time with him.

They held hands and walked north toward the town center, passing rows of shops, all to which Isla had seen Duncan make deliveries. Walking at his side, Isla felt more comfortable in this town than she ever had.

"You don't think we're rushing into this, are we? You meeting..." Isla's voice trailed off before she could say his son's name. It felt like the fractured parts of her life were coming together with permanent glue before she was comfortable with the way they'd been aligned.

"You can never move too quickly when a good thing is ahead of you." Duncan tipped his hat to a group of fishermen. Isla wondered if the two of them were thinking of the same thing.

"My mum once told me, 'careless feet are prone to stumbling,'" Isla said in a tone that made Duncan clench his fist and take a deep breath.

"Of course mothers preach caution. But I feel more comfortable with you than with anyone I've met in my life. From the day we met—"

Before he could complete his thought, Isla yanked his arm and they swung into an alley, their bodies meeting in an embrace. The damp wind swirled at their ankles. Isla couldn't pull her eyes away from his.

"Someone might see us." Duncan chuckled, his breath on her face. Their noses touched, and Duncan's hands clasped together at her lower back.

"Those were nice words of yours." Isla's gaze roved the crow's feet at the outside corners of his eyes, the dark freckles on his cheeks, the downward curve at the end of his nose. She detected a thought was circling in his mind, by the way his eyes narrowed and his mouth curled into a mischievous grin.

"You have a new idea, don't you?" Isla returned his smile.

"As a matter of fact, I do."

"Duncan Hester! Is it about your business?"

"Must we stop now? I'll explain myself when we get to our destination," he said without looking away, but she could tell he wanted to glance at his watch or his to-do list.

"Let's stay here a moment." She wished for this warm closeness to last, for their lips to touch.

"I have an appointment to keep," he said, releasing his grip.

Isla's face fell. "Carry on then. Don't mind me. I'm just glad I wore my walking shoes," she said good-naturedly.

They stepped back into the street and Duncan waved at a passerby. He was in quite a good mood, but also in a hurry as usual.

They found themselves in a mixture of activity at the next intersection. Crowds of long skirts, frilly hats and pleated trousers filtered past the bank and down the alley to the train platform. The tracks ran parallel to Main Street and stretched endlessly in each direction. Burly men, arms grayed with soot, shoveled piles of dusty debris off of a newly-paved section of road. Two elegant horses pulled a cart filled with wooden barrels past the bank, which was adorned with a sign stenciled with thin, gold lettering. A group of somber-faced women wearing plain dresses swished past, with boisterous children scurrying along at their heels. Everything seemed to be in flux, the sun's last light drawing families back to their homes and hungry stomachs toward supper.

Duncan stopped at a fenced-in area attached to one of the buildings and shook the hand of a tall, graying gentleman smoking a pipe.

"Ginger!" Isla rushed to the fence and stretched her hand to the stately horse on the other side, who greeted her with a gentle nudge.

"Langford led her here for me so we could walk on our own." Duncan nodded toward the other man, to whom Isla curtsied.

"I smell a conspiracy." Isla narrowed her eyes and placed her hands on her hips. Ginger whinnied.

"Not at all, ma'am." Langford puffed through a grin.

"Where is your appointment?" Isla reached for Duncan's arm. He froze as she pulled herself close again. "What's the matter?" she asked.

The look Duncan shot at Langford only raised her suspicions. She saw them glance furtively down the street, where a large, potbellied man with a red waistcoat and spectacles swaggered toward them from the train platform.

"This way, love." Duncan directed them down the fence line as he nodded back at Langford.

As curious as she was, Isla avoided turning to look at the spectacled man, and she held her tongue as they weaved through a crowd filing into a bar. Isla struggled to maintain her footing as Duncan forced them under the stone archway of a narrow store.

Isla hesitated as they stepped over the threshold. "We can't go in there. It's closed."

"The shopkeeper is expecting me." Duncan assured her.

Inside, shelves of knickknacks, colorful plates and tattered book spines lined the walls, and a maze of furniture, racks of fabrics, shoes and hats stood between them and a balding shopkeeper polishing silver with his apron. The thunder of an incoming train coming to a stop behind the building caused the china and silverware to rattle.

'Duncan, that must be them."

'We won't be a minute. I'm picking something up here for you." Duncan continued walking toward the checkout counter before Isla could respond.

'Good evening, Miss King and Mr. Hester." The shopkeeper reset a teapot on a beautiful wooden table. 'I heard you two have been seeing each other."

'You know Mr. Starling?" Duncan squinted at Isla.

'Miles visits the butcher every week." Isla was glad to surprise Duncan for once.

'Only the friendliest butcher in town," Mr. Starling said, showing large yellow teeth as his mouth stretched into a grin.

'I'm here to pick up the item you were preparing for me." Duncan stood at attention like a birding dog, his right arm bent behind him to retrieve a clip of money from his back pocket.

Mr. Starling cast a glance over each of his shoulders and frowned. 'I got carried away cleaning up the shop and time flew past me. You caught me off guard."

'He's been doing a lot of that lately." Isla ran a finger over a silk fabric and wondered at Duncan's surprise.

'Mr. Hester is on time for every delivery, and here I am lollygagging." The shopkeeper chortled as he waddled through the curtain at the back of the shop. 'While you're here, sir, could you take a new shipment request?"

'Of course, Miles." Duncan left a bank note next to the cash register and followed Mr. Starling to the storeroom. 'Just be a minute, love."

Isla twisted her lips and nodded. As the men disappeared, she recalled the sound of the train's arrival—would her sister wait for her at the platform? She shuffled to the shop's display window and peered out onto Main Street, which was now awash in the lampposts' glow. Fewer townspeople were milling about, their figures shadowy and moving steadily to their destinations. Only two silhouettes stood motionless, one towering and narrow and the other stout and rounded, both standing guard at the fenced pen. A moment later, Isla saw the outline of a woman and child, hand in hand, gliding past the bank. She cried out in delight and rushed to the door, but a hand snatched at her wrist and pulled her back.

"Wait a moment, dear. I have something to show you." Duncan's face was creased with anxiety, yet he seemed to be exerting great effort to seem cheerful and calm.

"Duncan, my sister is here. And Rangi."

It was the first time she had told Duncan her son's name. Maybe it would be better if she went out and greeted her sister and son on her own. Perhaps Duncan wasn't ready for this. She looked out the window again to see the newcomers walking toward the two men at the fence. Her stomach twisted at the thought of losing sight of them.

"Isla, please listen. I know I'm acting strangely—"

"I need to go meet them." Isla's body tensed in defiance.

"I was hoping for this quiet moment with you, before they arrive. You know how I get when meeting important people. This is a big deal, meeting your son."

Despite the tension boiling in her gut, a gracious affection swelled in her chest. "You'll do wonderfully, Duncan."

Duncan scooped her head into his hands and swept her face into his, lip over lip pressing in together. The muscles in Isla's neck and shoulders relaxed, and she let her head fall backward as Duncan kissed her again, her senses lost in the bliss of the moment.

They were recalled to their surroundings by Mr. Starling's forceful cough. Isla peeled herself slowly from Duncan's embrace and blinked rapidly, maintaining eye contact with her lover. What had just happened?

"Isla, love. You are so wonderful, so special to me." Duncan's voice was naturally soothing now. He continued to hold her hand. "The last two months have been an utter joy getting to know you. I'm so thankful you talked to me first that day at the shop. I was so awkward and witless."

Isla's head cleared enough for her to consider where Duncan's words were leading. Certainly, with her sister and son outside, the mysterious man at the horse pen, and the fact they had only known each other for a couple months?

"Duncan, I—"

Isla's attempted response was quieted by Duncan's finger. At the back of the shop, framed by the flickering light of a lantern, the shopkeeper held a box that could have contained a hat or a cake. She avoided looking at Duncan as questions swirled in her mind. She spluttered nervously, stepped backward, and then flew out the door and onto the cobblestone paving outside. She staggered toward the figures at the fence, convinced she heard a squeal or a cry. For some reason, her thoughts turned to the bloodstains on her gloves and white apron at the butcher, the messy, pungent carcass, the guts and fluids spilling to the floor at her feet.

She reached for her son, ignoring the interjections from the adults; whether they were greetings, protests or cries for help, she knew not. He was noticeably heavier, and he resisted as she lifted him into her arms. She kissed his neck, whispered in his ear, and then finally the blurring motion around her calmed and her sense of sight and hearing sharpened.

"Isla, you're a madwoman," Sylvia said as she gave Isla a brusque embrace. Isla's sister's black dress and brass buttons clung to her slight frame, and the scowl on her face was overshadowed by the wide-brimmed hat on her head. "I was worried when you weren't at the platform, leaving us wandering around in the dark. But the butcher scent led us to you." Sylvia's nostrils flared.

"I'm sorry to keep you waiting, Syl." Isla lowered Rangi back to the ground as he began to cry loudly. Sylvia swooped in to take him from her grasp.

"A pleasure to meet your sister, Miss Isla," Langford chimed in.

Isla attempted to fix her appearance, her face reddening in embarrassment.

The large man in the waistcoat made his presence known with a grumbling harrumph. "This is the strangest meeting I've been to. I thought Mr. Hester was with her," he bellowed.

Langford gestured toward the man. "This is Mr. Jameson, ma'am. He's one of Duncan's—"

"Business partners," Mr. Jameson interjected, extending a fleshy hand to Isla in greeting, which she gingerly shook. She was overwhelmed by all of the newcomers, but was most concerned about Rangi. She pivoted and tried to look at his face, which was now flopped over her sister's shoulder, his eyes closed.

"You don't look well, love," Sylvia delivered with a grimace.

Isla didn't respond, but instead ran her hand over Rangi's forehead. She felt everyone's attention on her, and then she sensed Duncan approaching, but she did not turn around.

Duncan greeted Mr. Jameson, followed by Sylvia and then Langford. Rangi's eyes snapped open. They were obsidian black, as rich and expansive as the night sky above. She saw the dancing reflection of the men interacting behind her as she looked into the face of the one who called her mother. She missed him.

A hand nudged her shoulder.

"Isla?" Duncan said quietly, as if just for her to hear. "Can I meet your son?"

She turned toward him. They looked at each other, acknowledging with their gaze their encounter back in Mr. Starling's shop.

"This is Rangi." Isla took the boy into her arms again and held him up for Duncan to see. She forgot about the strangeness of the other men watching them.

"Hullo, Rangi. My name is Duncan. It's nice to meet you." Duncan smiled, reservedly at first, and then with a toothy grin that made Rangi giggle.

"I have something for you and your son, I just needed it framed by Mr. Starling," Duncan said to Isla. He revealed the box from behind his back and showed it to Rangi.

Isla let the boy down and he lurched forward and touched the box, uncertain whether or not he could handle it on his own.

"Present?" Rangi asked.

"I made this for you, Rangi. What's inside." Duncan lifted the lid as Rangi nudged it with one of his fingers. The polished kauri wood became visible to the circle of onlookers in the orange lamplight. Sylvia gasped and Langford chuckled.

"It's beautiful, Duncan." Isla marveled at the circular carved patterns and flowing forms etched into the wood. On each side of the piece, an outstretched figure embraced a smaller form in between them. Rangi tilted his head and traced the shapes with his hand. As Isla inspected the artwork further, a lump built in her throat. She looked up from the wood.

"Why is Mr. Jameson here?" she asked.

"You have a way with your directness, my dear." Duncan stood, and Rangi retreated to take hold of Isla's legs. "Well, since you asked, I'm looking to buy land from Mr. Jameson out in Matamata, and we have been trying to come to an agreement. He came to give me an offer on Ginger and perhaps my business here in Hastings. Unfortunately, the timing did not work out quite as I had planned."

'It's not every day I come to meet a man about a deal and he immediately runs away from me." Mr. Jameson chortled.

Duncan laughed deeply, holding his stomach, his face crinkling in mirth. "You know I don't like being the center of attention."

The man standing before Isla continued to amaze her. This eventful, unexpected evening seemed like something only Duncan could cook up, even if Rangi and Sylvia's arrival had been a surprise to him. There were countless questions and protests she could fire at him now, but instead, she trusted him.

Isla looked down at her son. "Mr. Duncan is a kind man, Rangi. I love him very much. I'm glad you could meet him today."

Rangi peered up at her like the boy in the center of the wood carving—comfortable, sheltered and safe.

The Milkbar — Wharekai

Crusade on Queen Street

Auckland, 1950

Ron Hester remembered his last conversation with his younger brother, Wally, and felt his eyes twitch in sadness. He tried to maintain his focus by whispering a prayer of blessing for the chattering young people passing by on Queen Street, many of whom he recognized from University of Auckland campus. Ron surprised himself by briefly making eye contact with one of the girls from his biology class, a pant-wearing brunette with wide hips and a short, swaying ponytail. She squinted at him before quickly breaking her gaze and continuing ahead with her friends. He pushed his glasses up the bridge of his nose and adjusted his suspenders, wishing the tension in his neck would subside. He and two of his classmates walked in a single-file line at the edge of the street as the sun set on their backs. Crowds of young people walking in the opposite direction filtered into milk bars to drink and dance or continued down to the harbor to enjoy the twilight views. Cars honked at the trio as they tried to stay out of the travel lane.

Barry, an eager freshman, was lagging behind and spouting flippant jokes about some of the passersby. Art, a year ahead of Ron and in his last semester before graduating, hobbled in front of them, carrying a rough wooden cross he had nailed together with some pieces of a broken dorm bed. His broad shoulders sagged in exhaustion and he slowed down. Ron sighed deeply and tried to find a kind voice.

"Art, I appreciate what you're doing, but I think we can take a break now," he called above the clamor.

"Of course not. Seriously, Ron, it's the least I can do. This is my last few weeks here." Art sounded tired, but Ron knew from experience he was not going to give up.

Ron considered how effusively passionate his older sister, Anna, was about her faith. It had been her influence that guided him toward joining the Student Evangelism Crusade at the university when he moved to Auckland to pursue higher education. His mother also spoke often about the influence of her conversion to faith in her twenties, and Ron's father's consistent character and warnings of the world's ways gave him a hunger for a disciplined and active spiritual community.

Ron walked faster to catch up with Art, syncing his stride just behind the taller student. He thought of the Bible stories about sick people pushing through a crowd to touch the edge of Jesus's robe. Surely, Jesus was not as burdened as Art?

"Art, you've walked this street so many times trying to share God's love. You don't have to prove yourself anymore."

'I've walked this road many more times trying to find something to satisfy myself. Girls, drinking, dancing, getting in fights." The cross continued to bob up and down on Art's shoulder.

"I told you I had a story I could preach," Ron offered, wincing. He would have rather been holed up in his dorm room with a heavy book, but he'd told himself street ministry was his way of 'getting out of his shell.'

"I need to speak," Art said in a way that left Ron no room to respond. Ron heard Barry shouting at them to wait up.

"You see all these bodgies and widgies looking for a night on the town?" Barry laughed as he tugged at his expensive wool jacket, certain to be a hand-me-down from his businessman father.

"Who said it has to be you, huh?" Ron said to Art, forgetting about the students walking by for the first time.

"Whoa! What did I miss?" Barry interjected, trotting up to listen in.

Art stopped and turned toward Ron and Barry. "I'm not doing this for myself, or for you blokes. I'm doing this for the Lord, and for others to know him."

"Yeah, well you need a break. Look at you. You're worn out," Ron said.

"I appreciate your concern." Art drew a sharp breath. "But right now, I feel the Lord calling me to speak. I'm motivated by love, Ron. That won't wear out." Art's eyes were hovering on the crowd shifting past. He fiddled with the wood in his hands and lifted the cross slightly, as if to remind them why they stood there.

Ron gritted his teeth and tried to accept the scene. His dream from the night before flashed across his mind. It was him standing, surrounded by a crowd, speaking. And his brother was there, with his long hair, boots and a smug expression, taunting him.

"The story I wanted to share is fitting. The one I told you about," Ron said again, this time quieter, with his arms folded, pleading.

"Tomorrow, Ron. Please trust me." Art heaved the cross over to stand next to him.

Ron couldn't believe he'd ever looked up to Art. He'd even been jealous of his athleticism and handsome features, and how dramatic his conversion was. Now, his older classmate just seemed stuck-up and controlling.

"We're here to show 'em how different we are. That's what you said, isn't it, Art?" Barry cocked his head to the side and opened his arms, trying to lighten the mood.

"We're no better than any of these folks. They're just like us. In need of the Heavenly Father's love." Art spoke steadily, as if giving a eulogy. He looked each of them in the eyes, "Will you fellas pray for me? I'm gonna speak now."

Ron gave a quick nod and Barry slapped Art on the back. Ron pulled a pack of tracts from his pocket and shuffled through them. There was no way he was going to stand next to Art while he preached. He retraced their steps toward one of the milk bars, its neon sign flashing in welcome.

He noticed a group of young women in colorful jackets and jewelry who had gathered at a storefront nearby to watch the preaching trio. Rather than amused or disgusted, they looked curious. "Barry, come on, let's go talk to those ladies over there."

"Ooh, you see that cute blond girl on the right? She's a catch. Yes, let's." Barry elbowed Ron in the ribs and began to describe the girl who had caught his attention.

Ron looked at Barry.

"I know, I know." Barry shrugged sheepishly. "I'm still new to this."

"No, I'm not trying to make you feel guilty, just trying to..." Ron balled his hands together apologetically.

"But you looked at me."

"Yes, I did." Ron let his arms fall limply at his side.

"That reminded me that 'she's more than just what she looks like,'" Barry said thoughtfully.

"Well, yes, you're right." Ron looked around, suddenly wondering about his brother's whereabouts. He had no right to criticize Barry.

"And I'm a new creation in Christ. I can be different. I don't have to be horny," Barry concluded, grinning.

"Yes, that's true." Ron smiled weakly.

"Well, let's go then!" Barry hollered.

As they stepped up onto the sidewalk, they heard a commotion behind them. Some mathematics students in Ron's year pointed and laughed. Art had stopped and rested the cross on the paved street between his feet. He bowed his head and then surveyed the crowd. Ron felt a heaviness in his chest as Art began to speak with a loud, crisp voice laden with conviction. His chiseled jaw and commanding presence quickly drew a crowd.

"Come on, we're supposed to be talking to people," Ron said somewhat bitterly. He tried to drown out Art's words, but kept looking behind him to see his peer's speech ascend into a poignant soliloquy on the greatness of God.

Ron grabbed Barry's arm and walked further down the street, this time with the stream of young people. They stopped near the outer throng gathering around Art, a few steps from the group of girls.

Ron bit his lip and tried to be sensitive to a familiar tug inside of him. It reminded him of his mum's intuition to check on the neighbor down the road or to invite a hurting family over for dinner. He heard Barry begin to chat with the ladies they'd seen at the storefront. One began talking loudly in protest. Ron turned to see that Barry was guiding them through reading a tract, and one of the listeners' faces was pink in displeasure. Perhaps they were not as receptive as he'd thought. Barry's initiative was admirable, but he'd need some backup if they were to avoid a debacle. Ron walked toward them slowly so as to not catch them off guard.

"You mean to tell me that God wants me to burn forever? You can stuff that up your ass!" The frustrated girl shook her head and shoulders, her fancy leather jacket gleaming in the glow of sundown. They stood in front of a large window that reflected their doubles on the glass, next to a sign advertising ice cream, sodas, beer and hamburgers.

"Cindy, be quiet, will you? I'm sorry about her." The other girl lowered her long face and swept blonde bangs away from her eyes.

"Cindy, is it?" Barry asked.

The quieter girl nodded and added, "And I'm Sandra."

"Nice to meet you." Barry smiled, stood taller and pointed at the paper tract again. "Cindy, I was just like you, actually. I thought it was all a load of shit as well. When I was really lonely at the beginning of the year, I threw up a prayer to God but didn't expect anything to come of it."

Ron's chest tightened as he listened to Barry's spiel. This didn't feel at all like his father telling him and his siblings about colorful, flawed characters from the Scriptures after dinner by the fireplace, relating from his own life the perseverance of hard work, the pain of betrayal, or the risky choice to forgive and mend a relationship. Instead, this felt like being a cosmic vacuum salesman. Ron took a tenuous stride to stand beside Barry.

"Another one of you?" Cindy waved dismissively.

"Cindy, give them a chance!" Sandra gawked at her friend, who shot back a suspicious glare.

"Attagirl." Barry grinned and wiped the sweat from his brow. He grabbed Ron's shoulder and shook him. "This man was the answer to my prayer. He brought me alongside him and really showed me the ropes. He made God's love a personal thing in my life."

Ron merely waved. Somehow, Barry's words cut through his defensiveness in a way that left him speechless. Despite his brashness, something in Barry's story rang true, and Ron hoped it made their encounter more genuine than a sales pitch. Even still, he kept the pack of tracts tucked at his side.

"What gives you the nerve to come tell us how to live?" Cindy asked. She fiddled with the buttons on her jacket, a suit of armor she used for protection. Her freckled face continued to wrinkle in disgust.

"We're just here to share what God's done for us. We believe He meets us where we're at and invites us into a relationship with him. That's why God became a human—to be near us," Ron said.

"That's great for you. But people use God and religious stuff in all sorts of wacky ways to hurt other people," Cindy said.

Next to her, Sandra was still looking at the ground. The other girls in their group had walked into the milk bar. Ron lost his train of thought, instead picturing his brother's pained expression and the sense of justice Ron had felt the night he delivered the high-minded rebuke to Wally.

"Look, uh, we're not here to judge you, believe me. I've got plenty of faults of my own." Barry took a step back, but continued to talk with a warm smile. "I've heard fire and brimstone preachers and been yelled at plenty of times. But it was the love of someone being my friend that made me want to change and opened my eyes to who God really is." Barry pointed to the wooden cross now propped against Art's shoulder, barely visible above the crowd.

"We all need forgiveness," Ron murmured, remembering some lines he had practiced, written out in a notebook next to accounting sums. Forming phrases to articulate what he believed in, not wanting to rely solely on an impersonal piece of paper. "We are all capable of violence, hatred, lust, and envy. We need a way to become the people we were made to be, to be part of God's family."

Ron saw that Barry was eyeing Sandra again, who was stealing glances in return. Ron nudged him on the shoulder, but before Barry could get his next statement out, Cindy flapped her hand to cut him off.

"I wish you'd open your eyes and see you're being manipulated. The way I see it, you're just a boy who wants to have fun. And a good-looking one at that," Cindy said.

Sandra giggled nervously.

Barry leveled his gaze, and Ron winced in anticipation of the freshman's response.

"I appreciate the compliment." Ron thought he could hear Barry swallow. "Ron, do you have anything else to say?"

Ron remained frozen in place, wishing he had the courage to speak again. Words flew across his mind, ideas he had read in books and heard at summer camps, but nothing slowed down or made sense enough to turn to speech. He became terrified of what questions he would be asked, of how his life may be picked apart. Lost in thought, he didn't notice he had dropped the packet of tracts on the pavement until Cindy sniggered and pointed at his feet.

"Knock it off," Barry snapped, reaching for the fallen paper.

"This guy is just trying to control you. He's too scared to be out here on his own so he drags along someone else to do his dirty work. Why don't you come hang out with us, Barry?" Cindy threw her hair over her shoulder and batted her eyelids.

Barry was silent, and Ron avoided looking at him. Sandra inspected Ron for the first time, her eyes widening in alarm as if he were a fire-breathing monster in university student clothes. Barry finally mumbled a response, which Ron couldn't hear. The young man's face turned beet red as he glanced at Ron, his expression hinting at mistrust as his mouth formed into a frown.

"You're pathetic, both of you," Cindy spat, straightening her jacket with a swift tug. Sandra took her friend's elbow and turned away, as if to shepherd them toward the harbor down the hill.

Ron looked at Barry and grimaced. "I'm sorry." He shoved his hands into his pockets and felt his legs trembling.

With an exasperated grunt, Barry threw his tract at the girls as they departed and stormed off without looking back at Ron. The white piece of paper fluttered to the pavement as Barry's oversized coat disappeared into the crowd of students flocked outside the storefronts.

Ron pressed his fingers to his face. His throat felt like it was tightening as bodies pressed against his on each side. Art's voice had grown louder, and Ron swiveled to see a sizable crowd had gathered to listen to his sermon. The upperclassman was now standing on a bench, positioned like a town crier above onlookers licking ice cream cones and parents steering their children along the congested sidewalk.

Ron exhaled deeply, spun on his heel and walked into the milk bar at the corner, the one with the large red sign and the brand-new dining room; the one he knew well. At the end of the bar, he caught sight of the person he had expected to see. The hum of chattering voices inside seemed to exacerbate the anxiety raging inside him. The pinball machine squealed and rattled as he walked by, the jukebox shuffled between tunes with a click. As he marched past a busboy wiping tables, he fought the urge to turn around. Deep down, he wanted to run after Cindy and Sandra and smooth over their perception of him. He wanted to catch up with Barry and elaborate on his apology. Instead, he willfully marched along the shiny, gray-and-red-lined counter to the end of the shop, deliberately approaching two shaggy-haired students from behind.

"Wally," Ron announced, spinning one of the pair around by the shoulder. His breath caught when he realized it wasn't his brother; the occupant of the barstool was a girl.

"Watch it," the patron next to the girl cried. He swiveled around and yanked Ron's hand from the girl's shoulder. Ron found himself looking into the fiery blue eyes of his brother Wally.

"I'm sorry. I didn't mean to." Ron reset his glasses and looked between his brother and the girl next to him. Below her boyish haircut, her face was narrow with rosy cheeks, and her eyes were crowned with curvy lashes. Her pants were pulled tight at a high waist, but the bulky coat, blue slacks and heavy button-down shirt were analogous to Wally's appearance.

"No harm done." She rotated on her stool with an amused expression. "I'm Caroline. Are you Wally's brother?"

"He's leaving," Wally huffed, turning around to stick his nose back in the menu, although he had obviously already ordered and finished a large milkshake.

"Actually, Wally, I was hoping to have a word with you," Ron said, edging closer to let someone leave the toilet behind him. He felt cramped at the back of the milk bar with so many voices ricocheting off the walls.

"Please stay." Caroline gestured to the barstool that had just opened on her left. "I wish I could say I've heard a lot about you, but Wally doesn't talk much about his family."

Wally broke from the menu to glare at Caroline.

"Oh, piss off, Wally," she said, then smiled at Ron. "I'm his girlfriend, in case he never talks about me."

Ron fixed his suspenders and tried to hide the grin emerging on his face. His shoulder brushed against Caroline's as he sat. He couldn't bring himself to say that he hadn't seen his brother in months, but surely they'd spoken about it?

"Why are you here?" Wally asked, leaning forward to inspect his brother again. Judging by the auburn whiskers on his jaw, Wally had been avoiding a razor.

"I was down here for a drink," Ron lied. He folded his hands and looked at the soda fountain behind the counter.

"That's not like you. Were you part of the crowd out there?" Wally asked, his voice rising in suspicion.

"What's your favorite drink here, Ron?" Caroline ignored Wally's musings and showed Ron her menu.

'I love their ginger beer. We never had carbonated drinks growing up," Ron said.

'On a farm, right? Do tell me more." Caroline's voice was husky and calming. It was like soothing salve on his nerves.

'Down in Waikato, near a stream. Lots of pigs and cows and even some sheep for a while. It was heaps of work, but we did it together. Wally and I were in charge of a lot of it after our older siblings moved away. Took some convincing for our dad to let us move here for school." Ron could feel Wally looking at him.

'He's an old fella, eh? That's what Wally said. My parents have been in the city my whole life. It's not as exciting with your dad being a doctor," Caroline said with a melodious giggle.

'Cut to the chase, Ron. I come here almost every day and I haven't seen you since the first month of classes. Why are you here now?"

'Lay off it, won't you, Wally? I want to get to know your brother. It's the first time I've met him." Caroline took in the last sip of her drink with a scowl.

Wally spoke to Caroline in an angry whisper that Ron couldn't decipher over the noise of the loud bar. With a startling shake, she jumped off of her stool.

'God damn it, Wally, just talk to him, won't you?" She brushed her wispy bangs from her forehead and exhaled. With a bow, she gestured to Ron. 'Good to meet you, kind sir. I do hope you can work things out with your brother." She gave Wally, who did not move in response, a peck on the cheek and then sauntered through the busy bar to the door.

The two brothers sat in silence. Ron scooted over to the stool next to Wally's. The bartender came by and cleared Caroline's glass, but her smell still lingered.

'She's nice. And very cute," Ron said.

Wally did not respond.

"I did come with Art," Ron said after another moment.

"I knew it."

"Wally, I'm not better than you."

"Do you hear yourself?" Wally shot back. "Seriously, Ron? Do you have something stuck up your..." He turned back to his menu.

Ron fiddled with the hair pinched between his ear and the arm of his glasses. "What I was trying to say is I shouldn't have said those things the last time we were here. I know I'm gonna say it wrong again, but I don't care what you study, or how you spend your time. That's your business." He expected Wally to interject again, but when he did not, Ron continued his train of thought. "I... I care too much about the perception of things. I feel this jerk in my chest to judge things I think should be different, or to put up a front to seem a certain way to people." He felt a tear burning at the corner of his eye.

"To seem like you made something of yourself?" Wally sniffed. He rested his elbows on the plastic-coated menu and turned his head of wavy hair toward the other wall. "You made it clear that's what you expected the last time we were here. You don't have to say it again."

Ron reached out to touch his brother's shoulder, but he shimmied away.

"Wally, I was just thinking about Dad when I said that. About how we left him there without help."

"Shut up, Ron. Leave me alone, will you?"

"Wally," Ron pleaded in a raspy voice.

Wally turned and gave him the same look he had the last time at the milk bar, like a fighter in the ring knocked down for ten counts.

Ron walked back outside and saw the crowd had dispersed. A line of cars waited in traffic behind Art's silhouette. The burdened preacher had an arm around another young man, most likely Barry, whose body was shaking in sobs. In the hazy light of dusk, Ron caught a glimpse of Art's face. It was peaceful but still solemn, more relaxed now that he had delivered his message.

Gripped by a wave of unresolved pain, Ron let out an uncharacteristic cry. The pent-up energy flew through his foot as he kicked the red brick wall, his shoulders colliding with the bystanders scrambling out of his way.

Though bleary-eyed, he saw the white paper tract laying face down on the pavement. Without looking back at Art, Barry, or the milkbar, he stepped over the paper and strode back up Queen Street.

He hoped as never before that the paper's words, his beliefs, would somehow trickle down from his head and quell his angst. Somehow fix his relationship with his brother.

Fix his relationship with himself.

The Musterers' Hut — Māhau

Confessions in the Bush

Matamata, 1942

Their skin looked like burlap bags and white sheets draped over old furniture in the shadows. Wally wasn't one to snoop. As the youngest sibling, he treasured his privacy and made it a point to respect that of others. But the noises coming from the secluded musterers' hut in the bush behind their farm made him especially curious. Peeking between wooden boards nailed over a broken window, Wally's vision slowly adjusted. He saw piles of objects stored away, covered in years of disuse, all motionless save for one form—or maybe it was two—moving frantically about. He imagined it could be an animal, like the wild boars that dug in the mud down by the duck pond. But quickly he recognized the shifting shape was more humanlike.

There were muffled groans and cries, and he worried if the person may be hurt, until he distinguished both his brother Joshua's voice, followed by a girl's voice he knew was not his sister's. The fuzzy hair on his arms bristled as he realized their moans were in pleasure. His stomach lurched when he saw thin white fingers clutching at Joshua's bare back. Until this uncomfortable moment, Wally had been feeling proud yet envious of his brother since he'd returned for university break. The scene playing out before him solidified just how much Joshua had changed. Wally wondered at his brother's bravado as he spoke to this girl, and the way she reacted to him. He was both sickened and entranced as he stared through the wooden slats. His brothers had made sure to teach him all of the slang terms for love-making, but if this was what they referred to, he certainly wanted nothing of it.

The pair's movement transitioned further into the dark as they leaned back on a pile of animal skins Wally was sure smelled foul. He saw the girl's feet kicking, and she giggled as Joshua's pants flew into the light, casting a spray of dust into the air. Wally covered his face with his arm and tried not to cough.

"Joshua, are you sure we're alone?" his brother's girlfriend whispered.

"There's no one around. It's our little secret," Joshua said.

A cloud of shame seeped through Wally's skin, clawing at his throat like the dust from the hut floor. He squeezed his eyes shut and stepped back from the window. Memories swept through his mind and he almost lost his balance.

He thought back to the farmhand his dad had hired a number of years ago, before he was old enough to know what was happening. He bowed his head and whimpered, suddenly frightened by the secret of being alone with that man against his will. Even more painful was how friendly the interactions were at first, until eventually it was impossible for Wally to distinguish his genuine desire for attention from the exposing, forceful, and deceitful nature of the hired farmer.

Wally turned and ran down the hill, oblivious as to whether his brother heard him. The trees moved past in a blur, and he stumbled twice on hidden rocks and fallen limbs. He had no idea where to run to, and even less of a clue of how to escape the painful images resurfaced in his mind. His senses were overwhelmed and he considered collapsing on the hill, tumbling down it like a log split for the fire.

It was his sister's voice that pulled him from his distress. Anna's sobs were quiet and subdued, as if hidden by her usually collected and approachable demeanor. But Wally could tell she was distraught. She sat in a heap on pieces of fence that had been bowled over by an animal. His head was still throbbing and his thoughts cloudy from what he had witnessed at the hut, but his heart moved for his sister.

"Ann?" Wally used her nickname. He wove through a group of trees to stand next to her. She gasped and looked up at him.

"Wally! Oh, bugger. You always know my hiding spots don't you?"

"What's the matter, Ann?" It felt like his chest was tied with a rope someone tightened from behind. He crouched down beside her.

"I'm OK, really." She smoothed her ruffled skirt and sat up straight. Her face was still a little red and puffy, but otherwise she now looked composed. Despite himself, Wally chucked in admiration of his older sister.

Anna finally spoke again. "Well, I've been home for a day and I've already started an argument with Dad."

"Really? You actually talked back to him?" Wally sat down on the toppled fence post next to his sister. For a moment, he almost forgot about Joshua and the ugly memories.

"Yes, I did. I wanted him to understand my point of view. I realized that as the oldest, I put a lot of pressure on myself to do what's expected of me. But this time, I needed to share my dreams with him, even if he doesn't like them."

Wally figured she had a point, which made him think about all the hoops he jumped through as the youngest sibling. He also knew she called herself the oldest out of habit, even though Rangi, their half brother, was actually a few years older than her.

"Was he giving you a hard time about your job?"

"Actually, I don't have one at the moment. That's the problem. I stopped my part-time work to focus on my teaching certificate."

"You would be good at that."

"Pardon me?"

"At teaching. I can see you doing that."

She looked at him for a moment. "Thank you. That's very kind."

"I don't see why he wouldn't want you to be a teacher."

"Well, it's not that simple. Please understand, I'm not trying to speak bad about our father. And I know he works hard to make ends meet. But..." Anna stopped and pursed her lips, leaning back to look up at the dense foliage overhead.

"What is it? Did you ask for money?"

"Yes, yes I did. But it's not just about the money. I know Dad's not perfect, but he's usually fair and has the utmost integrity. And I never want to pit us siblings against each other. But I have worked my way through school and didn't ask for much, while Dad paid for all of Joshua's university fees, and he hasn't even been working. And now Dad said I have to pay for my training myself."

"I'm sorry."

"And if that isn't enough—I'm not complaining, just trying to explain my side—Joshua announced he's dropped out of school to go to Australia next month, and Dad said he'd pay for his travel, because he's doing a stint on an oil rig. Meanwhile, I want to go overseas to do mission work when I finish my training, and Dad told me he doesn't like the idea."

Wally felt overwhelmed by his sister's predicament.

"It's because I'm not a son." She slumped her shoulders and parted her lips, puffing air upward and scattering the hair from eyes.

Wally frowned. This didn't sound like Anna.

"Goodness, sorry. I shouldn't have said that." Anna smothered her face with her hands. "He loves me, I know he does. In his own way."

That sounded more like her. Never making a big fuss, always looking on the bright side. Even so, Wally had not given much thought to Anna's experience as a daughter, and how it differed from his experience as a son. He sensed a new crack form in the mental image he carried of his father, leaving a fracture he could not easily repair.

"It's OK," Wally lied. "You didn't mean it."

"You don't look so great either. Are you sick?"

"Kinda feeling that way." He pushed his folded arms tighter against his stomach and leaned forward. "Anna, I ... I need to say something, too."

"I'm sorry, Wally. I've been chattering away. What is it?"

He squeezed his eyes shut and felt his heartbeat shuddering through his limbs. He was aware of each part of his wiry frame—his toes in his tight shoes, his backside on the rough wood, his throbbing stomach, the growing pains in his arms and legs, his back doubled in pain, face pinched together, his private parts. All wrapped in a weight of shame that yanked him from his body, as if he were staring at it from the outside.

"I, uh, got hurt a while ago," he said softly, his eyes still closed. "Someone hurt me."

The cryptic yet honest words forced Wally's eyes open. He saw concern radiating from his sister's face.

"Where? When? Who?" She leaned forward, as if to force this information from him by close proximity.

"Just let me speak."

He began to share, the words spilling out of him as he described the man who used to work at the farm. He closed his eyes as he recounted the first time the man touched him inappropriately. Anna's eyes widened and her body stiffened. Wally knew that she, as he once had, suddenly understood the man's ulterior motives. The frightening images came into stark focus. Wally considered for the first time the man's violence toward him. It was not a brutal kind, but a sinister taking of his innocence.

'It was my fault." He blinked and took in the fuzzy trees around them as heavy tears rolled down his face. 'I could have fought. I could have not gone with him and been alone."

'No, no, no. Wally, you didn't do anything wrong, you hear me? That was...just terrible, horrible what he did to you."

'But it happened again."

As he opened up about his experience, it was difficult to be completely honest, or to know exactly when to stop telling the horrid stories. He felt comfortable in his sister's presence, but found it was almost as if he were talking about another person's experience in order to protect himself.

Anna continued to apologize profusely as she stretched her arm across his shoulders and pulled him into an embrace. Wally didn't really hear her words, he just felt her body against his. The thought of Joshua and his girlfriend crossed his mind. He was ready to recoil from his sister, but instead, he stayed, feeling comforted, seen, heard. This was family.

'We should go talk to Dad," he heard her say. His chest tensed again, and he shook his head emphatically.

Anna craned her neck to make eye contact with him. 'Wally, thank you for sharing with me. But I think—"

'I'd rather talk to Mum."

'I understand, Wally, believe me. But you should—" Anna stopped herself. 'It may be harder, but I think talking to Dad would be the best for you. As a man."

'Well, you can't make me."

'No, of course I can't. You've been violated, Wally. But you've also been brave enough to share."

'It's not just about me sharing. It's how everything changes once I talk about it. How people will see me. I didn't want to tell you, but I just had to, like I would have exploded if I hadn't." Wally felt his face burning, as if he were stretched under the heat of the sun.

"Now he has less power over you."

"Yeah, it does feel like that."

Anna nodded. "I know from experience, too. The world isn't kind." Anna looked down the hill, toward the farmhouse. "Sometimes those closest to you can end up hurting you the most."

The secret of his abuse weighed on Wally less, but now he thought of Joshua again. Would his brother regret having sex in the musterers' hut? Did the girl really want to be there with him? It made him blush, but it sounded fun, passionate. Right now, however, he felt a pain in his gut about the thought of being naked with another human. Should he confront his brother about his actions, or did he have to keep another secret? Would Joshua receive the news of Wally's abuse as graciously as Anna had? What about the other members of his family?

The leaves at their feet crunched as Anna stood, her skirt swaying as she ambled down the slope.

"Where are you going?" Wally rubbed his abdomen.

"To talk to Dad," she called without turning back.

"No, Anna, you can't!" Wally shot up, feeling betrayed.

"Wally, I need to talk to him." She turned and glared at him, but her eyes hinted at her good intent. "I think I realized more of his perspective, maybe more of his mistrust. You inspired me."

"Can I come? To make sure you don't tell on me?" He joined her halfway down the slope. He was almost as tall as her now, but not nearly as grown-up as his older sister.

"Tell on you? How many times do I have to say I won't?" Anna smiled, finally. "Yes, yes. Come on."

The Card Game — Kēmu Kāri

Manhunt at the Bach

Te Aroha, 1961

The domed lamp over the card table swung in circles, highlighting each face gathered below it at odd intervals. The wood-paneled walls of the small sitting room seemed to tilt endlessly, giving Joshua the sensation of being at sea. Even though he was seated in a remote, run-down bach at the base of the Kaimai mountains he'd just purchased with oil rig money, it felt like he was again on the boat carrying him away from his fractured family in Australia and back to his Waikato childhood.

Joshua tugged at a tangled patch of his auburn beard, inspecting his brothers over the ten playing cards fanned in his hand. Ron was stoic as usual, only betraying his emotions when looking doe-eyed at his son, Lance. The baby was now much too big to be constantly held, but nevertheless, Ron sat across the table with Lance asleep on his lap, the scent of a soiled nappy hanging in the stagnant air. Wally occupied the third chair, chattering on about their weekend itinerary at the bach, which was in a state of flux due to a heavy rainstorm. Wally's lean, hairy frame buzzed with distracted energy. He drummed his fingers on the table and continuously turned back to the kitchen, as if he could see through the wall to check on their father. It was a toss-up to Joshua if having his brothers and father here for a weekend was worth the unnecessary noise and confusing brushes with his past.

He stared at his cards again and sipped on a bitterly warm beer. His brothers hadn't made it through one round of bidding in their game of 500 without folding. They either had lousy cards or were willfully apathetic. Still, he had brashly bet on winning seven of the ten tricks. With one black jack, ace and joker, Joshua decided to take a risk and call the trump suit spades. He laid the ace of hearts on the table as the starting card of the game and then rested his chin on his fist.

"You two actually gonna play? It's no fun going against a pair of mannequins." Joshua shifted in his chair and crossed his arms, letting his fanned cards tilt to one side, but he had no concern of his brothers stealing a glance.

"We're here, Josh. We're playing," Ron said over the whistling wind buffeting the small window at his shoulder. He rubbed his balding head as he bounced Lance on one knee.

"Wally?"

Wally blinked and gave a swift nod, even though he was now looking up at the lamp hanging from the ceiling.

"You play the next card, Wally. You're to my left." Joshua scratched behind his ear and then took another swig of beer.

"I wanted Dad to join us." Wally tossed the king of hearts into the middle, and Joshua couldn't help smirking at the fact his brother had wasted the second-best card in the suit.

"Dad hates cards. He doesn't like betting," Ron whispered in a patronizing tone, though he was not the oldest brother. But then again, neither was Joshua.

"He has a keen eye for strategy, you know. I think he would enjoy it if he tried," Wally said loudly. Ron gave him a look of warning as he played a low heart.

"What? He's sleeping now. I can tell," Wally said. He looked over at Joshua, who was now collecting the three cards, having won the first trick. "You were the one most keen on him coming, Josh." Wally tapped on the table again.

'He's not himself." Joshua formed the three cards into a neat stack. He felt sick to his stomach, and he tried not to think about the shell of his father snoozing in the next room.

'It was good of you to invite us here, Josh," Ron said graciously.

'I do wish Rangi had made it," Wally muttered, after which Joshua felt the stir of Ron delivering a swift kick to their younger brother under the table. Joshua decided it best not to mention he hadn't invited Rangi.

'I suggest you two find some strategy of your own if you're gonna keep me from running away with this game," he said, tossing his black jack into the middle.

As they took turns each playing a card, Joshua easily won the first few tricks.

'Do you run your business like this?" he taunted, playing his joker on the empty table and then watching as Wally and Ron revealed cards that had no chance of winning. He swept up the cards into his win pile and played a lower trump card without hesitation, which Wally wasn't able to beat.

'We do OK for ourselves," said Ron, laying down the queen of spades with a confident flourish. Wally whooped and pushed the three cards from the completed trick to Ron's side of the table.

'Bloody hell. What was I thinking?" Joshua spread his long fingers over his eyes and rubbed his forehead.

'Ron runs a tight ship," Wally quipped, ignoring Joshua's anguish. 'We make it work with just four employees."

'And Wally's brought in heaps of new contracts." Ron reached for the lamp overhead and the room became still. 'Speaking of business, have you found any work here, Josh?"

'Does it look like I want to talk about that now?" Joshua grumbled. 'I'm trying to focus."

'It's just a game, Josh. We don't have to keep tabs," Wally said in the mild-mannered, diplomatic voice that was quickly getting on Joshua's nerves.

'I've got plenty of money. That's not what I'm worried about." Joshua looked down at the five cards left in his hand, the game half over. He chewed on his lip, thinking through the domino effect of playing each of his remaining cards.

Lance stirred with a groggy whimper, his shiny blond hair creating a halo around his bobbing head.

'We're almost done, Lance. Bedtime soon," Ron whispered into his son's ear. Lance whined in response, pulling at a toy bear on the table.

'This game's not done yet. I've still got you blokes." Joshua tapped his foot against the table leg and watched the room rattle again. In his peripheral vision, he saw Lance's face turn beet red above his powder blue jumper. With a squeal, the child swiped at his dad's cards, knocking over a glass of water that rushed across the table like an incoming tide. Wally pounced forward in an effort to clean up the mess, and Ron spun around to dry off Lance and scold him. By the time Joshua lifted himself from his chair, the lamp had begun swinging again, and he flopped back down in a daze. The chaos in the tiny room was suffocating, reminding him of living in Adelaide, being pulled apart by his three children and wife and ground to a pulp by long yet lucrative hours at the oil rig. Like he was thrown into a pit and left for dead. Or maybe he'd tripped on his feet and stumbled in by his own doing.

'Mommy," Lance cried, tugging at Ron's neck as soon as they were reseated at the table.

Ron shushed his son and lifted him up over his shoulder, patting Lance's small back. 'You almost woke up Grandad, little man."

"I'm going to check on Dad." Wally maneuvered behind his chair along the wall toward the kitchen.

"Wait, Wally. Finish the game, will you?" Joshua insisted, jabbing his finger at the table.

Wally called to their dad to convey that their game was almost over. Satisfied at what sounded like a grunt from the kitchen, Wally seated himself and took a deep breath. Joshua cracked his knuckles and tried to think only about the game in front of him.

After a few more tricks, Wally had won two and Joshua was up against his bet. He looked at his two remaining cards and weighed his options, balling his fist so his fingernails dug into his palm. It was nearly impossible now to win the seven tricks he'd bet on.

"Looks like you've both lived a little more than I thought." Joshua tried to sip from his empty bottle. He threw it on the floor next to four others. His head was spinning.

"Wally taught me how to play 500 during our downtime at the shop," Ron said as if explaining a school subject, while holding Lance's head under his chin.

Wally shrugged. "I played with some of my mates at university."

Joshua threw an utterly average card onto the table, incensed at how the game had no effect on his brothers. With his eyes turned down, he saw a shadow creep across the table, and he sensed a figure walk into the room. His brothers did not react. The new presence moved with too much agility and stealth to be their father. It was like a dark cloud in their midst, straining the orange lamplight to a muted gray. Joshua felt the familiar tug of guilt in his chest like gravity, as if someone were slowly pulling the chair out from under him.

Joshua looked up to see a young man standing over him. Hair hung over his long, swarthy face, and he wore a heavy blue coat and canvas trousers. Even through the grime smeared on the boy's face,

Joshua recognized his eldest son. Patrick did not speak. His face was blank and eyes glassy like he had just witnessed a crime.

Joshua laughed through his nose, scoffing at this mysterious, impossible occurrence. The other two expressed their confusion.

"Suddenly in a good mood? Or accepting your fate?" Ron leaned over and tossed his card into the middle, revealing the missing trump card and winning the second-to-last trick. Lance cooed.

Joshua hit the table and stood up, his head colliding with the lamp. The light swooped around, revealing that Patrick was gone. The muscles in Joshua's neck tightened like vice grips. His son was no longer in the small sitting room, but Joshua still felt a haunting chill down his spine.

"For Christ's sake, Joshua. Grow up a little." Wally pushed the cards he'd won into the middle of the table.

"What are you doing? We haven't finished," Joshua growled.

"From your reaction, I think we have," Wally said, frowning.

"Cut it out you two." Ron held up his hand. "Dad?" he called, lifting his chin like a hound on a scent.

A creaking noise echoed from outside, followed by what sounded like a closing door from the kitchen. Wally rushed to the other room, and after a beat, Ron followed, standing in the doorway to survey the kitchen.

"He's gone! And the front door is ajar. How the hell did he get out without us hearing?" Wally's cry was pinched, as if someone were at his neck.

"Calm down, Wally. He probably just went for a walk." Joshua gathered the cards into his hands, breathing slowly to keep from being triggered by his brother's overreaction. Wally wiggled around Ron to face Joshua.

"Not when it's been pouring rain and he has a bad leg. Mum told me not to leave him alone." Wally peered out the small window in the sitting room and then marched back to the kitchen. "I'm going to look for him."

"Take a flashlight, Wally," Ron called.

As Wally scrambled out the door shouting after their father, Joshua carefully shuffled the cards and chuckled. "He just went out for a smoke." The edges of the cards felt like worn leather on his fingertips.

"He doesn't smoke anymore." Ron buckled at his knees, bobbing up and down with Lance on his hip.

"Well, good on him. But you don't have to keep reminding me I haven't been around." Joshua stood up and stretched his back.

"It was because of Lance, I think." Ron seemed to ignore Joshua's protest. "Dad has really changed recently. Not just his memory. It's like he's more relaxed, like he has a new vitality to him."

Joshua couldn't keep track of all the versions of his dad he was hearing about and experiencing in such a short time. He turned out the light above the table.

"Why aren't you out there with Wally?" Joshua grunted.

"You know him. He gets restless and can't stay still for long. He couldn't have gone far."

Joshua walked around Ron and shuffled out to the kitchen, scowling as he looked over the room. It smelled like freshly brewed tea and musty clothes, likely due to the water dripping from the ceiling near the front door. He shut off the stove burner and emptied the water collected in the pail below the leak.

Out the window above the sink, Joshua saw the dancing glow of the torch scanning the grounds like a lighthouse in an earthquake. The muscles in his neck relaxed for the first time since his dad had set foot in the bach. As much as he'd wanted Duncan to join them, sharing the space with his dad had kept Joshua on edge. He felt for the list of questions in his pocket. He had written them in a feverish scrawl, only a few of which he could bring himself to ask his dad, but none of which Duncan could be expected to answer in his current state of confusion.

Joshua fell backward into the patterned easy chair where Duncan had been napping. His brother was right, the chair was free from the smell of tobacco Joshua always associated with his dad.

Wally's hollering after their father grew more distant.

"I'm going to check on them." Ron retrieved his jacket from the coat closet, threw it around his shoulders in such a way as to shield Lance as well, and stepped out into the night to join the search.

Alone with his thoughts, Joshua's eyes lingered on the narrow closet near the front door. He reached for a packet of biscuits on the table nearby and munched nervously, unable now to avoid worrying about his father. The shadowy void of the closet was like a blank canvas on which his fears spilled their ink: his wife on the hospital bed after his intoxicated rage, angry letters in the post from his children across the Tasman Sea, his siblings and parents standing shoulder to shoulder like a firing squad to condemn him.

Joshua sprang to his feet and rifled through the hanging coats and empty boxes in the closet, clawing all the way to the back wall. He felt the wooden grooves of his hidden gun rack—it was empty.

Unable to breathe, he staggered back from the closet. Memories flooded his mind from a summer years ago on the farm when his father had pulled a dusty shotgun from under his bed and marched red-faced up the hill to fix Joshua's drunken mistake. Joshua suddenly felt like he was back in that moment, in the hormonal rages of his teenage body.

He scanned the room again, looking for signs of his father's movements this time. Duncan's boots were missing from the pile of shoes at the front door, and the mug on the kitchen table was still full of tea, the tea bag string hanging out on one side. Beside the mug was his father's Bible and a journal filled with his tiny, neat handwriting. A small book of pictures lay open to a black and white portrait of Joshua and his smiling siblings lined up along a fence. Their mum had sent the album with Duncan to help jog his memory.

On the adjacent page, a photograph of an elegant stallion looked to be freshly torn at the edges, as if it had been forced from its slot. As Joshua stepped closer to the table, the photo became like a portal to the past. Midnight had been Joshua's coming-of-age responsibility, and the envy of his mates and siblings. He was a small yet handsome horse, much too elegant for manual labor but just right for showing off to girls. It was Joshua's careless ride down the steep, rocky trails that mortally injured Midnight, his fate sealed by Duncan's shotgun. Joshua felt his eyes burning and he tried several times to swallow.

The room in the bach spun again, even though there was no domed lamp swaying above. As if on cue, the lights in the kitchen went out with a sputter. Joshua pounded the back of the easy chair with his fist, sending biscuit crumbs flying from the fabric into the air. He was alone in the dark.

He hated to imagine the worst, but he couldn't help himself. What drove his dad outside with a shotgun? Duncan was not a hunter. The weather was horrendous, night had fallen, and Duncan's aged mind was obviously impaired. Joshua had only seen his father brandish a weapon in great danger or when he was provoked by his incorrigible son's folly. The photo of the stallion was seared on the back of his eyelids as he rubbed his forehead incessantly, cursing himself for being so self-absorbed and ignorant of the state of things.

In a daze, he retrieved a lantern from the closet and trudged outside, fumbling with a match to light it. The rain had stopped, but he tugged the hood of his poncho on and wiped the snot from his mustache. He circled the rectangular frame of the bach, his head pulsating with each step, hoping he would not hear a gunshot. To Joshua's great relief, his beat-up red ute was still standing in the gravel drive next to Ron's small Toyota. The piles of sticks he'd gathered before the rain were strewn across his path. It wasn't difficult to picture Duncan looking for a walking stick in his hazy yet determined state of mind. But the question remained: where was he headed?

'Decided to join us?' Ron's voice came from the other side of the driveway, where the ground sloped away to a ditch that trickled down to the main road. Lance gargled and extended his small fingers out toward Joshua as Ron walked into the lantern light.

'Where is he?' Joshua croaked.

'We haven't seen him.' Wally's torch flashed into sight. His face was creased with concern.

'You look like you've seen a ghost, Josh,' Ron said. 'It'll be OK. We'll find him.'

'I reckon we call into town for help.' Wally stepped closer and spoke calmly, even though his body was jittery with anxiety.

'The power went out,' Joshua said.

'Christ!' Wally cried, turning his back on them.

'Not a bad idea to ask for his help, too, Wally,' Ron said.

'Quiet, you two.' Joshua held out his arm in a protective stance and lifted the lantern overhead.

A silhouette drifted behind his brothers, beyond the halo of the lantern's glow. Joshua stood taller.

'Dad?'

It was Patrick again, his shadowy face calm now, even pleasant, but again no one could see him but Joshua. An animal noise caused them to jump in fright.

'Let's go inside,' Ron said.

A cup of tea did little to settle Joshua's nerves and imagination as they took up different perches in the kitchen.

'So what's the plan? Do we wait here until morning?" Ron said from a chair in the corner of the room. Lance had finally fallen asleep again, the boy's miniature frame slumped against his dad's chest. A lit candle flickered in the middle of the room next to the photo album still open on the table.

'No, we can't do that. He won't remember where he is. He's not safe out there." Joshua paced, talking into his hand as he repetitively smoothed his beard. He was afraid to leave anyone at the bach on their own to face a harried Duncan armed with a shotgun.

'You two can go. I'll stay here with Lance," Ron said in a whisper.

Wally reappeared with another lantern. 'I agree. We'll move faster if it's just the two of us." He swung a sack around, which he filled with various items necessary for a manhunt.

Joshua felt the hairs on his arms bristle. He spun around and saw Patrick again, standing in the doorway, his eyes brooding and intense. It was the same look he had given Joshua just months ago when Joshua left him and his sister, Julia.

'I want you with us, Ron," Joshua said, turning his back on the vision of his son.

'Lance doesn't need to be out there," Ron said, more sternly this time.

'For crying out loud, what were you thinking bringing him here? This was supposed to be *our* trip." Joshua found himself gesturing in the heat of his emotion, his arms expanding out like a bird of prey.

'He's my son, Joshua." Ron folded himself over Lance like a nursing mother.

'He's an infant."

'He's almost two years old."

'Can he protect himself? Can he contribute anything?"

Ron's eyes narrowed. 'Since when is that a prerequisite to be part of this family?"

Joshua turned away. He knew the words had a bite to them, underneath what Ron was really trying to say. Wally grimaced. The room was quiet.

'I'm sorry, Joshua. I didn't mean that." Ron's voice wavered. 'What I meant to say was—"

"That you don't want to be here?" Joshua said.

'It's not like that, Joshua," Wally piped in. 'We want to be here. We came to spend time with you. But now we need to find Dad."

'Of course I know that! But I want us together. What was Mum thinking sending him here?" In his peripheral vision, Joshua saw Patrick take a step into the kitchen.

'It was your idea, Joshua. You said you wanted to hear more of his stories." Wally tossed some fruit into the sack and rapped on the counter with his knuckles.

'Yes, well now the crazy bloke is on the loose and I have to protect all of you!" Joshua looked between his brothers, but they would not return his gaze. Wally continued packing, even as his arms shook visibly in anxiety or anger.

'He's not a maniac, Joshua, he's just losing his memory. I'm worried about him, not scared of him. And now it's been at least an hour since he went missing. We need to get on his trail." Wally's chest was heaving now, and his face was flushed red. It occurred to Joshua that he might look the same way.

Ron stood up and shifted Lance over to his hip, his body facing Joshua's across the room as if in a quick-draw duel. His voice was measured and firm, like a radio announcer, when he spoke.

'And if you must know, Joshua, my wife is sick. Very sad kind of sick, to where she stares out the window for hours but won't talk. Yesterday, she left town to go to her mum's for I don't know how long. She's in no condition to be a mother, so Lance had to come with me."

Instead of turning away, Joshua let the weight of the agitated silence in the bach settle over him. The burn of Patrick's stare on the back of his neck seemed to close his throat, preventing him from responding to his brothers.

Wally paused his frenzied packing to pat Ron on the shoulder, then he opened the narrow closet and retrieved a pair of gum boots and a rain jacket.

"Do you have a gun, Joshua? The rack looks empty." Wally swung the closet door in and out, the squeal of the hinge rattling Joshua's skull. He was caught off guard by Wally's discovery.

"We'll all go on the hunt. Not another word about it," Joshua said, yanking the closet door from Wally's grasp and shutting it himself. He looked back at the doorway to the sitting room.

Patrick had disappeared.

~ ~ ~

The moon illuminated the wooded hillside with a silver glow. Joshua, Wally, and Ron trudged through a hazy curtain of mist floating downward in waves from the tree canopy. Joshua ignored the chill of the moisture clinging to his face and beard. Instead, he felt a surge of confidence leading the others up the track. It was cathartic to feel the strain in his thighs with each stride up the steep slope. The cool night air filled his lungs like a fresh sea breeze into an empty sail. This was the adventure he was looking for.

Periodically, Ron called ahead for him to slow down, in response to which Joshua heaved his shoulders and sighed in a dramatic fashion. Lance, who was bundled in a makeshift wrap on Ron's back, kept his head peeked over his dad's shoulder in an effort to observe their shadowy environment. Silver ferns fanned like volcanic eruptions over the narrow track up the hillside. Rivulets had been carved into the reddish brown soil, tracing the path of rainfall to the stream running behind the bach.

Wally shone his torch on a muddy portion of the track. 'I think I see footprints. Someone's been tramping up here recently."

"They could be anyone's," Ron said. 'I told you, Dad wouldn't have come this way, it's too steep."

'I recognize them. They're Dad's boots," Joshua said. 'He's moving quickly, but we're gaining ground."

In reality, until seeing the prints he had only been half sure of Duncan's route. Ascending the hill gave them a better vantage point if nothing else. A clearing at the top of this hill would provide a panoramic view of the valley below, and Joshua expected the waxing moon to highlight Duncan's position, unless he'd ascended too far above them. Joshua had made quick work in the last few weeks of familiarizing himself with the valley, and he hoped his knowledge of the land would give them the advantage. Still, with adrenaline and paranoia clouding his judgement, Joshua had to keep reminding himself they were not trying to hunt an animal, just find their father.

'How come you don't have a dog?" Wally asked. He had to repeat himself to get Joshua's attention.

Joshua scoffed. 'Hell, I don't know how long I'm staying here. Why should I have a dog to care for?" He tore back a prickly pine branch in their way.

'It would've been helpful to catch Dad's scent. Besides, you need some company," Wally said.

"The quiet has done me good."

'Don't you miss your family?" Ron said.

Leave it to Ron to say something so direct, Joshua thought, like letting his hand show in a rematch of 500.

'I didn't leave on good terms."

'I gathered as much." Ron's response was hampered by heavy breathing, but Joshua could detect his disdain.

'It's none of your damn business."

"My niece and nephew and sister-in-law are. And my brother."

Joshua swung around and felt his fists and abdomen tighten like a reflex.

'Leave it, Joshua," said Wally, grabbing Joshua's sleeve to keep him from rushing down the hill at their brother.

'Let's keep our eyes open and our traps shut," Joshua said through gritted teeth.

They silently took in the view at the top of the hill. The muted gray valley below was punctuated with glinting lights from streetlamps and houses like sparse constellations. Mountain peaks loomed over them like giants sleeping on their sides. Gaps in the trees down the slope revealed the outline of the path they'd followed up the hill, and over to the right Joshua could make out the next reach of the track as well as the main road below them, which led to the neighboring town.

'I can't see him," Joshua said after a few minutes.

'Looks like the lights didn't go out in Te Aroha, so it must have been a downed tree close by that took the power out," Ron observed.

"This reminds me of the hill above the musterers' hut back in Matamata, past the corn field. The one with the shepherd's track up the side. The view was similar." Wally swept the torch lazily across the rock outcroppings around the crest of the hill.

'I caught you and Caroline snogging up there the first time you brought her to the farm." Ron laughed.

'It's a nice spot." Wally shrugged.

Ron passed Lance to Wally as the pair continued their reminiscent chatter.

A flash of memories transported Joshua back to their childhood farmland, to the paddock over the hill where he'd taken Midnight on the ill-fated ride.

Joshua lifted his lantern and walked in a wide circuit, scanning the rippling grass at his feet for signs of Duncan's trail. The clearing extended out toward the base of a rocky cliff, where Joshua remembered seeing cave openings during his last visit. The shape of the rocks did remind him of the hills above the bush behind their old farmhouse. Shadows accentuated the form of a humpback, the profile of a wolf, and an elephant and her young hidden on the walls of the cliff.

He nearly tripped on a tangle of vines that had been pulled away from a rock pile. Intrigued, he followed the vines, which crawled along a fissure in the rock that widened into the mouth of a cave. Was his dad still moving or could he have sought shelter here?

He yanked the vines back further and ducked into the cave opening, dismayed to find the lantern light barely broke into the blackness. He could sense from the movement of cold air that the cavern went down rather than forward, down into the heart of the mountain. It was ludicrous to think his dad had chosen this route, but intuition beckoned him into the dark.

"What are you doing in there?" Ron called.

Joshua spun around, but lost his footing, slipping down into the cavern opening. He felt the loose rock give way and tear at his pants as he slid. Grasping at tree roots with his free hand, he was relieved that his boots found a ledge just a few feet down.

"I'm OK, don't worry. I thought I heard something," Joshua said. "Keep looking for footprints and see if he went around the bend."

His brothers chastised him for being careless, but their idle chatter resumed as they wandered around the clearing.

An urgent voice echoed up the throat of the cave, pulling at Joshua like a hand out of the hidden depths. It sounded like his own voice, brash and booming, but younger and terrorized—Patrick's voice.

"I'm coming!" Joshua yelled without thinking. Certainly it wasn't his son. It was Duncan who was missing. But he heard the voice with his conscience, not his ears.

A frayed rope snaked over the ledge at his feet. Curious, he pulled at it, and felt an equal force at the other end. Setting the lantern on a rock shelf, he gripped the rope and heaved upward. His footing gave slightly, so he widened his stance and leaned forward, as hand over hand he pulled the rope up from the bowels of the cave. Stone powder filled the air and his breathing became ragged, but he still heard the cry from below.

A minute later, he sensed someone at his shoulder.

"I found Dad's hat!" Wally cried. A tan, wide-brimmed hat flew in front of Joshua's eyes.

"Out of my way," Joshua growled in warning.

Wally gasped. "He couldn't be down there, could he?"

"Joshua, get out of there," came Ron's voice.

Joshua grunted again, as much in pain as in determination.

"The hat was near where the track picks up again. We saw a walking stick, too. He must have kept going up," Wally explained.

The new discoveries did not deter Joshua's focus. The rope continued to collect at his feet, and the weight on the other end felt heavier as his muscles ached in protest.

"What's gotten into you? Dad's not down there," Ron said, covering Lance's face from the dust.

"I heard a voice," Joshua insisted.

Suddenly, there was a rattle against the rock face, and Joshua felt the rope tremble. After a few more tugs, he could distinguish a form emerging from the darkness below. It swayed about like an energetic child but was much smaller than a person.

"A bucket?" Wally moved the lantern light to reveal the wooden pail now in Joshua's hands, water sloshing over the side into the cavern.

Joshua inspected the reflection staring back at him in the pail's contents. The face was wrinkled with anger, the eyebrows arching in disgust. But as the surface of the water rippled, a different yet familiar face greeted him. He could not tell if it was one of his children, parents, siblings or his wife, but it exhibited emotion like the colors of a chameleon, each expression full and genuine. The face laughed with mirth, mourned in tears and then finally returned his gaze with a powerful conviction that caused Joshua's legs to weaken.

He yelled, not unlike the mysterious cry from below, as if his current, disappointed self was calling to his curious past self for rescue. With a violent movement, he threw the wooden pail, which ricocheted off the cave wall and sent chunks of stone flying in every direction.

Ron and Wally called to him, but Joshua couldn't make out their words. Patrick's voice was no longer distinguishable, either, as layers of dust fell like sheets.

Rocks pelted Joshua from above, colliding with his skull and breaking skin.

The lantern light went dim.

~ ~ ~

Joshua awoke to the warmth of a fire. Ron sat with his back on a rock, poking at the smoldering logs with a stick. Lance was still bundled in the padded sack next to his father. The stars twinkled above the grassy hilltop, no longer hidden by rain clouds.

"You're fortunate that cave didn't swallow you whole." Ron stared into the fire.

"Did you find him?" Joshua gingerly touched his face, too sore to sit up.

Ron shook his head. "Wally kept going up the track to find Dad's footsteps."

Joshua swore. "I thought I made it clear we need to stay together."

"Why are you so paranoid?" Ron's voice was strained, but the marbleized orange glow obscured the emotion on his face. "You could have died back there. You're lucky we were able to pull you out."

Joshua didn't answer. He was tempted to test Ron's anger, until it dawned on him how Ron's responsible personality was a greater burden than Joshua had ever carried.

"Why did Dad take the gun, Joshua?" Ron sounded desperate for answers now, as if he knew his brother was not being forthright.

"I don't know," Joshua lied, though he was worried about Wally's safety.

"What was that in the cave?"

"Nothing." Joshua sat up, ignoring the fierce pain coursing through his head.

"You risked your jolly life for something in there." Ron tossed the stick into the fire, which billowed in response.

Before Joshua could lash out in anger, he saw Patrick again, this time inside his bruised head instead of a vision outside it.

"I thought I heard my son," Joshua whispered, reflecting back on the surreal encounter in the cave.

"Patrick? Here?"

"Don't ask me to explain. But I can't shake the feeling he's following me, trying to get my attention."

"What do you reckon he wants?" Ron said after a pause.

'So you don't think I'm crazy?"

'No, Joshua. He's your son. Half the time I'm worried about how I've failed Lance as a father, and he's only two."

'I think Patrick's trying to tell me to come home." Joshua rubbed his hands together.

'Have you talked to him lately?"

"The last time we spoke, he said he never wanted to see me again. And I was OK with that. He and his sister wanted to be with their mum, and I was done with Australia. I was done with that life."

'If you reach out to him again, he may have changed his mind," Ron said gently. 'Though maybe you have to decide first if *you've* changed your mind."

The brothers watched the flames dance without looking at each other.

'You're a good father, Ron," Joshua said. The words rushed over him as he said them, like a tide returning out to the ocean.

There was a tear in Ron's eye when Joshua finally glanced at his brother over the fire's glow. Ron's lips quivered, then sputtered into a laugh. With a quick movement, he pulled his hands over his face, emerging a second later wearing a contorted grin.

Joshua felt a warmth in his chest as he returned Ron's grin with his own, pushing his cheeks in with his thumbs and waving his palms outward. The volley of wacky expressions continued, and before long Ron and Joshua were on their feet using even their arms and legs to outdo each other's goofy gestures.

Wally emerged from the bush and trotted over to the fire, panting. 'What the hell?"

'I think I edged you out, Joshua." Ron clutched his sides as he laughed. Joshua protested by playfully punching his brother's arm.

'I thought we were looking for Dad." Wally's arms were folded.

'Oh, knock it off," Joshua said.

"You're sounding an awful lot like our older brother, Wally," Ron quipped, eliciting another punch from Joshua.

"I saw Dad's footprints farther up the track," Wally announced, his face ashen. "And I heard a gunshot."

Joshua and Ron were abruptly pulled from their childlike exchange.

"Are you sure? I didn't hear anything," Ron said.

"I went over a ridge, so the sound may not have traveled. But I know I heard it. I would have kept going, but the track split into two directions, so I ran back to get help."

Joshua had hoped his dad would stop before the fork. He could picture the ridge Wally mentioned, and the steep slopes on each side of the track as it crisscrossed down the back side of the hill to the valley below.

"Did you see another bach?" Joshua asked, thinking of the cavern well he'd discovered.

Wally shook his head. "But there was a fence line halfway down that seemed to mark out paddocks. And I think I saw some horses."

Without another word, Joshua put out the fire and rushed them up the track. Overhead, the sky began to turn reddish gray.

When Wally asked about Joshua's cave experience, Ron gave a blessedly simple explanation on Joshua's behalf. Then the two began arguing over what their dad could have been shooting at.

"I think it's my horse." Joshua spoke up, cutting them off. "And no, I didn't buy one," he added before Wally could ask.

"You mean he's been triggered by a memory of Midnight? I thought he loved that horse," Wally replied.

"He did. There were pictures of him in the photo album Mum made him," Ron attested.

Joshua felt the weight of secrecy clawing at his throat again, but he coughed it away. "I guess he never told you about Midnight's death," he said.

"He was injured, wasn't he? I remember Dad taking it very hard," Ron said.

"I rode him too hard when I was a teenager, showing off for my girlfriend. I'd been drinking and was up on the rocky pass above the farmhouse, jumping over fallen trees. Midnight was pushing against me, but I kept forcing him on, until he wrecked his ankles and then got caught in a ledge and thrashed about, hurting himself even more. I ran back to get Dad. It all happened so fast. Next thing I knew, he trekked up there with the shotgun and..." Joshua gasped for breath as they reached the top of the ridge. The view over the side was a welcome distraction.

"That's terrible," said Wally. "No, he never told us that."

"You didn't tell us either," Ron said ominously.

Joshua didn't respond. Instead, he let his gaze follow the now-visible wooden fence along the track ahead, which sectioned off a tract of rolling hills and a watering hole, bordered by dense bush beyond. The pre-dawn air was humid and carried the buzz of cicadas.

"Are you afraid he's still angry with you?" Wally asked, taking a step forward to stand in front of Joshua.

"He trusted me with that horse. I want to believe he cares about me, but there's a scary, untamed side of him that's etched into my mind. Most of the time I don't know which version of him is true." Joshua squinted at the tree line ahead, looking for a light or movement, acutely aware of his brothers' focus on him as he stood in between them.

"Is it fair to see him that way?" said Ron.

"What if we just do? He's our dad; he's shaped us for the better and the worse," said Wally.

'I think it's more for the better," said Ron.

"Well, now you know why I'm afraid of the missing shotgun." Joshua walked past Wally down the track.

'I told you, he's changed, Joshua. Anger doesn't control him anymore," Ron said.

"Old age does strange things with the mind," Joshua replied.

He stopped again to inspect a group of horses approaching them in the growing light. They appeared unfazed by the brothers' presence, yet remained a stone's throw away from the fence, perhaps to compensate for the mysterious gunshot. The largest of the group had a long, black mane, a white star and stockings, and held Joshua's gaze without flinching. With a respectful nod, Joshua turned back, letting his brothers pass so he could walk behind them. He found himself unable to shake the strength of the horse's scrutiny.

Lance stirred as the brothers continued on, approaching the fork in the track. Ron removed his son from the backpack and let the toddler walk alongside him, careful to avoid the muddy pools along the track.

'Look, more footprints," Ron said.

"And they're going off the track!" Wally ran ahead to inspect and then waved over to the bush, above which golden sunlight now burst forth.

Squinting into the sunrise, Joshua froze as he heard gunshots echo through the trees. The following moments were a blur. Joshua yelled instructions as he scrambled up the steep slope to the tree line, his brothers and nephew close behind.

They made three paths into the bush, hoping to remain within earshot of each other. Like his encounter in the cave, Joshua felt an invisible force drawing him through the trees like a magnet. As rough branches whipped across his body, Joshua was reminded of a conversation with his dad back at the farm, the day Joshua was the first child to leave home. He remembered the look of fear in Duncan's eyes, the Achilles' heel in his otherwise enraged demeanor and fit of angry curses. Joshua had remained silent, head bowed, patiently waiting to walk out and never return. He was strong, much stronger than his old man, and braver, too. He didn't have to hide in the hills when there was an entire world to be seen and experienced. Looking back, something about that moment felt sacred. It was the closest he had been to his father's raw emotion and interior world, and Joshua had felt powerful being able to take it, to unflinchingly listen and not yell back, to respond only with a shut door. But now, crashing through the trees in search of a shrinking old man, Joshua longed to face his father again, to raise his head and look him directly in the eyes, to wait until the tears came, to somehow recreate the "home" he had left in too much haste.

He wanted to go back to the truck in South Australia and tell his daughter and son that he should never have yelled at their mother or laid his hands on her in anger. To take Patrick out fishing, and Julia for a ride on the back of his motorcycle. To do anything he could to earn his wife's trust again.

He wanted to sit across from his brother Rangi and just listen. To let him say anything he wanted, to take it. He knew it would take a lifetime to start over. But maybe there was still a chance.

Joshua saw his dad's body down the slope, his legs splayed like the broken roots of a fallen tree tearing the earth out from below. He keeled over and found himself on his knees. His arms quivered and his back tightened in shock. He touched his father and was relieved to discover there was no blood on him. His father's face was peaceful, slack, and still.

"Dad," Joshua whispered.

"Joshua." The voice was slow, gentle.

Joshua mumbled, unable to form words—to scold his dad, to apologize, or to make light of the situation. He bit his lip and gripped his father's frame, cradling him like a soldier on the battlefield.

"Where are we?" Duncan's eyes were glazed over.

Joshua moaned. "I won't leave you. We'll get you back home."

"Don't carry on, now. I won't fall apart on you. I had a job to do. I just took a bit of a fall I guess."

"Where is the gun, Dad? What did you do with it?"

"You know I don't carry a gun around the farm." Duncan gave a coy smile.

"But you've been..." Joshua searched Duncan's face in confusion. He appeared tired and disoriented, but not angry.

"Son—" Duncan fought through a labored cough. "I was too hard on you, wasn't I?"

"I'm sorry about the horse, Dad." Joshua choked back tears.

"You're a good man, Joshua." Duncan looked at him knowingly, deeply. Kindly.

Joshua placed his head on his father's chest and cried. At first, Duncan's body remained tense, but after a moment, his hands were combing Joshua's hair and patting the top of his son's head. In the shadows of the early morning light, Joshua made out the form of the shotgun barrel protruding from a pile of leaves down the slope.

Ron's and Wally's calls filtered down the hill, mixing with the sound of Joshua's sobs.

~ ~ ~

His father's words remained in Joshua's ear long after Duncan left the bach with Wally, Ron and Lance in Ron's Toyota the following day. The old man did not seem to remember the events of the previous night, and thankfully he didn't have any bruises or broken bones from his fall in the bush. Ron insisted he would tell their mother about the escapade, but Wally assured Joshua he would paint the story in the best light possible.

Joshua stashed the crumpled list of questions for his dad in a kitchen drawer. He hated to be a coward after a moment of such clarity, but there was only so much emotion he could handle after a morning of weeping in front of his dad, brothers and nephew. In time, he would ask them.

With his dad's permission, Joshua kept the photo of Midnight. After the others left, he spent the afternoon at the card table carefully writing its story, letting the flat image deepen into a multilayered, emotional tale on lined paper. He enclosed the pages and the photograph in an envelope addressed to Australia.

That night, he dreamed of riding horses with Patrick in the hills above the farmhouse.

The Car — Motokā

The View from Outside

When Isla surveyed her daughter, she saw the distinctive features of her late husband. Anna's dark, frizzy hair was pulled back in a braid, her narrow brown eyes were directed down at a book on her lap, and her pointed chin was wrinkled in reaction to the story she was reading. Isla had hoped that having her company on this impromptu trip would fill the void of widow loneliness she carried. Instead, as the swaying fir trees and lush hills swept past their train car window, Isla was finding it even more difficult to stymie her anxious thoughts than at home. It wasn't fair of her to expect so much from her daughter.

Isla adjusted in her seat and resumed the zigzag in her warp knitting pattern, forming the red yarn into small, tight loops as she tried to calm her breathing. Isla held out the half-finished jumper for Anna to admire her progress, to which her daughter gave a small nod and then returned to her book. Squaring her shoulders, Isla couldn't help feeling the phantom of Duncan's hand in the small of her back. Instead of a comfort, it caused her stomach to lurch, as if she were clutching to the underside of the train car. She hoped Anna would hear her pathetic murmuring and say something.

A short, mustached man in a blue-rimmed hat and brass-buttoned waistcoat stopped in the aisle and leaned over them, clearing his throat. *"Kia ora*, ladies. Tickets, please." He placed a wrinkled hand on the back of the seat, much too close to Isla's shoulder.

Isla collected their tickets and passed them to the man without making eye contact.

"What's taking you to Palmerston North?" The conductor punched their tickets and made no effort to keep the chads from floating onto Isla's ruffled, white blouse.

"Good day, sir," Isla said in a small voice, her chest tense and her knees squeezed together.

The man's hand did not move. He shifted in his spot and took the tickets from the passengers in the next row.

"We're going to visit my brother," Anna said in a cheerful tone.

The conductor leaned in toward Anna, his coat nearly brushing against Isla's squirming nose.

"Will you stay long?" His breath was a pungent mix of Earl Grey tea and honey.

Isla lifted slightly from her seat, causing the conductor to topple backward in reaction. "Thank you, sir. That's enough of that. Kindly move along."

"What's gotten into you, Mum?" Anna asked. She looked up at the bewildered conductor and gave him an apologetic smirk, before he continued more briskly down the aisle.

Anna returned to her book.

"Won't you talk to me, love?" Isla said after a beat.

Anna wore a curious expression as she raised her face. "You feeling more like yourself, then?" Her eyes squinted above a half smile, one of her dimples displaying prominently as she clasped her hands over the closed book in her lap.

Isla drew from the deep well of her thoughts. *Am I a good mother? Do you see me as one?* Isla considered it an utterly selfish question to ask, so she kept it to herself. "Let me ask you something about yourself," Isla said instead.

Anna giggled with a loud squeak. "Ask away."

"What was it like leaving home?" It was a question that had been brewing in her psyche for ages, haunting the annals of her motherhood. One she hadn't had the courage to ask until now.

"Moving back to Matamata?" Anna replied.

"No, going to Africa."

"Wow, that came from out of nowhere. That feels like a long, long time ago." Anna turned to stare out the window. The bright sunshine made her face clearly visible in the glass, like a silent observer of their conversation.

"You're not that old. Don't forget who you're talking to." Isla shook her head sourly.

Anna swung back with a grin. "You'll be young forever, Mum."

Isla's tiny chortle was drowned out by the rumble of the train's engine. The tightness in her chest subsided as she placed her hand on her daughter's face.

"I will never forget that day we said goodbye to you in Auckland, when you left on that frightening airplane. You were going away to some distant jungle, to people with a completely different language and way of life."

"Kenya's mostly grassland and desert, Mum. And there are plenty of people who speak English." Anna removed her mother's hand from her face and smiled playfully.

Isla was dismayed at her daughter's dismissive reaction. "But you didn't know that then." She tilted her head and lowered her voice. "Why did you go, Anna?"

"I knew I was supposed to go." Anna bit her lip and looked up at the luggage overhead. "It felt like I was already overseas and I had to go and catch up with myself. I had worked toward it for so long. God had a mission for me there. It sounds so high-minded now, but I just felt like it was my destiny."

"I know it was important to you." Isla rested her head back on the seat and tried to process Anna's words. "Youth is a heady experience. But when you're young, it's the easiest to move."

"You did. And even younger than I was when I went overseas, right?"

"I had to, but for different reasons. I was a widow. I wanted Rangi to be near family, but I needed to breathe, and I couldn't do that in my hometown with everyone staring at me, expecting me to cry all the time."

Anna took Isla's hand into hers. "That helps me see you as another person, not just my mum," she said after a moment's silence. "Do you feel that way again, like you need more space to breathe?"

"I'm in a completely different season of life." Isla swallowed and kept her hand limp, unable to keep herself from trembling. "But yes, I am sad."

Anna rested her head on Isla's shoulder.

"I should have gone with you," Isla said.

"To Kenya? You didn't even want *me* to go."

"I didn't want you to be alone. And I didn't want you to be so burdened."

"How could you have come with me with what was happening on the farm? Joshua leaving, then Rangi, then Ron and Wally."

"Of course it wouldn't have been practical. But it's the feeling a mother has. You'll understand one day. You can't control it, like your desire to leave and find yourself." Isla smoothed her blouse and felt the muscles in her face tighten. "Even so, a part of me traveled with you. I thought of you every day. And when you came back, I wanted to latch on to you, but you had changed. You were your own woman."

Anna turned to her reflection again. "Those were really hard years. It's probably not what you want to hear, but I didn't think about home much. I think I had to block it out to get through everything I experienced in Kenya. I wasn't the same when I got home."

Isla sighed. "What has come over us?"

'Being on the road does it to you. I don't think we've ever traveled together, just the two of us," Anna said, looking at her mum again.

'It's like we've been to a confessional."

"A widow and her spinster daughter, coming clean."

Isla felt a pinprick in her chest. The weight of uncertainty returned like a sack of feed on her shoulders. She fished the yarn and needles from her bag and began to knit again. She sensed her daughter was still willing to talk, but she needed to do something with her idle hands, something familiar that she could control.

"Do you think of Rangi every day, like you did when I was gone?" Anna asked, her book still untouched in her lap.

'Yes, of course." The needles in Isla's hands looped around each other efficiently, like a machine. 'It's not right that we've been apart so long."

Anna edged closer to Isla. 'What will you do when you see him?"

'Smile, say hello, and give him a hug if he'll let me." She completed a row and turned her work over, the small success bringing a short breath of relief.

'He'll be at the station to pick us up, you know," Anna said slowly.

'How..." Isla let go of the needles and tried to gauge Anna's demeanor in her peripheral vision.

'I called him this morning and asked. I couldn't keep it a secret any longer."

'Why didn't you tell me you'd spoken to him?"

'Wally gave me his number. They've just started talking again." Anna fiddled with her braid, her brow furrowed.

Isla pursed her lips and eyed her watch, unwilling to reply.

'Don't be that way, Mum," said Anna. 'Everything has moved so quickly the last few weeks. I thought it was better he knew we were coming, and that you weren't worrying about it needlessly."

Isla pulled her bag up onto her lap and looked at her daughter for a full minute.

'I told you about the letter he wrote back to me after I sent news of your dad's passing," Isla managed to say without her voice cracking. 'It sounded like he was struggling. I didn't think he'd have a phone, or a place for us to stay. I was going to ring a motel when we arrived."

'Why didn't you ask him?"

'It would have taken too long by post."

'I just think you have the wrong impression," Anna whispered tentatively.

'You should be glad I invited you." Isla buttoned up her bag.

'Yes, I am glad," Anna said curtly, peering out the window at telephone lines and a cluster of green farmhouses.

With an exasperated screech, the train rumbled into the Palmerston North station. The large orange overhangs along the platform sheltered them from the setting sun as they disembarked. Isla struggled with her three bags as they descended from the platform to a gravel car park. Anna formed their luggage into a pile.

'How long do you reckon we'll be waiting?" Isla adjusted her stockings and watched as a few families ran across the tracks toward the town center.

'I think that's him there." Anna shielded her eyes as she pointed across the car park, her smile flashing in the sunset's glow. A car honked and Isla nearly dropped her bag onto the ground in shock. A midnight blue Plymouth Fury swung around in front of them, spitting gravel in its wake and reflecting their mound of bags and incredulous expressions in its shiny, chrome hubcaps.

"Rangi!" Anna cried, keeping her arm against her forehead as she circled the pristine car to the driver's side.

Isla was unmoved as her son emerged from the vehicle, which remained idling with a constant, full-throated hum. Anna stopped short next to the boot of the car and stretched out her arms in a greeting.

Rangi's dark eyebrows were curved upward, and he glanced furtively between his mother and half sister. His gray-flecked black hair was slicked back like a helmet, the ends curling up over his collar, a scraggly beard obscuring the lower half of his face. As he moved from behind the car, Isla saw one of his arms was decorated in distinctive Maori tattoos. He was only a ghost of the son she remembered, sporting a confident new demeanor and style she did not recognize. She watched in a daze as Anna approached Rangi with hesitation, until suddenly her son rushed forward and gathered his sister into an embrace, spinning and swaying her like a ballroom dancer.

"Good to see you, Ann!" Rangi's face melted into a soft expression.

Anna pulled back and let out a squeal, which spilled over into a humorous retelling of a childhood memory. Isla silently looked on from next to the pile of luggage, still clutching her handbag and spinning her wedding ring with her thumb. Her vision blurred as she shifted her weight back and forth between feet. She felt like a train conductor observing her passengers, not privy to the relational bond in the platform reunion.

"Hello, Mum." Rangi's greeting pulled her from her trance. He lumbered toward her, his hands now tucked into his pockets.

"Hi, Rangi," Isla replied instinctively.

Her firstborn son stood before her, graying, a middle-aged adult. Her eyes burned, bulging from her face as tears threatened to burst forth. She held on to her bag like a life preserver, the rush of memories a white water river raging below. With a quivering breath, she deliberately blinked a few times, and then found herself staggering toward Rangi, whose arms gently enfolded her.

"I'm so sorry, Rangi, love. I should have come sooner." Isla kept her arms at her chest, still holding her handbag.

"Mum, it's OK. I'm OK. I'm glad you're here." He tilted her face with his calloused hands and looked into her eyes. "I'm sorry about Dad." His lips were pressed together into a hazy line like the horizon behind him.

Isla nodded. She stole a glance at the clouds above and shook her head to clear away the desire to weep.

Rangi hefted their luggage into the spacious boot and carefully shut the hatch, then helped them into the car, Isla insisting that Anna have the passenger seat next to her brother. Anna's mouth was agape as she ran her fingers over the stately gray interior.

"I know what you're thinking. No, this isn't my car. I'm borrowing it from my boss. I could never afford it," Rangi said, certainly blushing under his beard.

"I couldn't even imagine myself driving this, let alone owning it." Anna sighed.

"Goodness me. I raised a family of narcissists." Isla laughed airily. She gasped when she felt the crisp leather deflate slowly as she eased into the back seat.

"Just wait till you meet my boss. He's a real character. He's very fond of himself." Sliding behind the steering wheel, Rangi guided them out of the car park and onto the main street passing through the town center. The inside of the car smelled like freshly peeled orange, like sitting in the grass in the citrus grove behind the old farmhouse in Matamata. The memories traveled quickly through Isla's mind, flooding in as Rangi drove the car over the train tracks.

'But he's taught me a lot, my boss, from accounting to repair work to sales," Rangi continued, speaking quickly. 'I think he might be offering me a management position soon."

'That's wonderful, Rangi!" Anna gushed.

Isla didn't register Anna and Rangi's chatter in the front. Instead, she took in the white and green-fenced yards along their route, the smoothly paved roads and the rich orange sunlight scattering from the metal roofs on the handsome houses. She could have been floating in a cloud along streets of gold, the stately elm trees shading her view of the pearly gates ahead. Her eyes wandered lazily from the manicured street grid to her children. Rangi's face was fixed ahead, but his cheeks were pulled back into a grin, and Anna's braid flew like the tail of a kite in the breeze from her open window.

Before long, the car careened into a driveway and stopped under the shade of a carport. Flowers bloomed along a winding walk to a modest yet well-kept cottage. This was certainly not at all the neighborhood in which she'd pictured Rangi living.

'Mum? Did you hear Rangi?" Anna gripped the back of her seat, her face flush with enthusiasm. 'He said he's going to be a father!"

Yet again, Isla's mind was thrust into a liminal state. She had resigned herself to the idea Rangi, like Anna, would not have children.

'I'm sorry I didn't tell you sooner. I decided to wait until you got here." Rangi gave a sheepish shrug. 'You're going to be a grandmother, Mum. I mean, you already are, but again, eh?"

'She likes to be called Nana." Anna looked at her brother with childlike glee. 'Rangi, I'm so happy for you!"

'It's a lot to take in, I reckon." He delivered a sideways glance toward his mother.

As the engine stopped with a shudder, they were greeted by two giggling girls, their silky black hair and slender limbs flailing in all directions. Rangi leaped from the car and simultaneously caught ahold of their waists, hoisting them into the air.

'Esther, Constance, meet your Aunty Anna and Nana." Rangi's beard nuzzled into their giddy faces. The girls' eyes twinkled at Isla, wooing her into their spell. They waved bashfully, all the while appearing comfortable in Rangi's arms.

A slender woman appeared at the edge of the path, holding her swelling abdomen as she bowed deferentially. Her hair was jet-black like the girls', and was held neatly behind her narrow face in an elegant red clasp.

'Mum, Anna, this is Megumi." Rangi froze as if in awe, letting the girls slide to the ground. 'Esther and Constance's mum, and my partner."

'Hello, nice to meet you." Megumi smiled at them, while at the same time casting her gaze on the two girls and balling one fist at her hip so that they came to attention and rushed to her side.

Isla sensed she had crossed into this woman's domain. Megumi's collected, respectful exterior contained a commanding presence.

Anna and Isla bowed at different intervals, uncertain of the best way to return Megumi's greeting. The small woman laughed like a breeze across a wind chime, which set them at ease. Rangi took Megumi's hand and kissed her cheek. She closed her eyes as her face creased with joy.

'May I?" Anna asked, her fingers reaching for Megumi's belly.

The pregnant woman blushed and took a step forward. 'She is only a few weeks away." Megumi's cheeks were still flushed, but she looked at Rangi with a slight frown. The group was quiet for a moment, except for Anna's delighted murmurs as she felt the baby's movement.

'Would you like to feel, too?" Megumi's English was clear, almost without a foreign accent, unlike Isla's initial assumption.

Isla held out an unsteady hand and touched the flowery skirt wrinkled over the woman's protruding middle. She felt Rangi's gaze on her, Anna's hand on her shoulder, and Esther and Constance tugging at her clothes for a better position among the adults. Isla was beyond being surprised now; each moment was like a new step into a busy marketplace, overloading her senses.

She returned her hand to her side and swiveled around to retrieve her suitcase. One of the girls guided her inside by tugging at her sleeve. They brushed past dahlias and roses, whose bursts of color were like the waning sunset overhead, and in a single-file line the group shuffled into a small lounge. Rangi and Megumi buzzed around the room with as much movement as the children, turning on lights, gathering chairs and tidying toys and papers.

"Take a seat, Mum." Anna gestured to the sofa near the window. Isla dropped her bags and sat at the very edge of the cushion.

"Would you like a cup of tea?" Rangi asked as he threw a kettle on the stove without waiting for a response.

"Look at our artwork!" The younger of the girls, perhaps Esther, brandished a paper with colorful hand-drawn patterns. Soon, a series of pages flew by Isla's face: flowers, houses, birds, and a family of stick figures. Isla took one drawing and stared at the large, bearded face of her son surrounded by a mother and her two daughters, their heads brimming with numerous penciled hairs.

"Girls, come get ready for bedtime. They'll still be here in the morning," Megumi said firmly, placing a mug of tea on the table next to Isla. Rangi hung back in the kitchen as Megumi herded the children down the narrow hallway.

Anna yawned and rested her hand on Isla's arm, which continued to clutch the drawing. As Isla stewed in thought, she resented that Anna did not seem to sense the tension in her shoulders and the discomfort in her posture, but instead remained quiet, maybe even with closed eyes. However, surely Rangi discerned Isla's unease, his wordless stare keeping track of her inspection of the sitting room, maybe even aware of her conflicted judgement of her son. What was wrong with her?

"How's the tea, Mum?" Rangi took a few steps and hovered in the lounge for a moment, breathing deeply.

The mug sat untouched on the table. "Thank you, Rangi. I'm sure I will enjoy it. I just have a lot on my mind. I'm still adjusting to your new life here. It feels so different. Comfortable, but much different than I was expecting." Isla could feel Anna moving forward on the sofa. Rangi appeared to shed the confidence he'd carried earlier at the train station. Isla felt justified yet ashamed for being so forthright. She lifted her voice to complete her thought. "I wish your dad could see you now. I miss him."

"Of course. If you'll excuse me," Rangi said after a beat, then he disappeared down the hallway.

"Mum." Anna's voice was raspy.

Isla stood and walked to the door, but was stopped in her tracks by a collection of items she hadn't yet noticed. On a small table draped with a patterned gray fabric stood a rich, mahogany wooden rectangle propped against a stand. The wood, carved by Duncan's hand, depicted a familiar scene of two curving figures embracing a small child between them. Behind it was perched a wine-colored, wood-paneled radio set, its knobs and dials worn by Rangi's use. Beside the radio was a golden frame with a faded photograph of Rangi's father, Thomas King, wearing wool soldier breeches and a hat overshadowing his eyes. The sight of these artifacts transported Isla through the memories of Rangi's childhood. As if from the heavens, she considered the influence of the two husbands she'd survived, the way her son's life had been affected by each of her decisions and the tragedies outside of her control.

She walked outside to the concrete path. The flowers still smelled sweet, and the darkening sky was a deep blue like the Plymouth in the driveway. The sounds of the night were punctuated by passing vehicles and the neighbor's television set.

"Aren't you happy for him?" Anna called over the loud clash of the shutting door.

"Of course I am," Isla said in a low voice as she folded her arms and looked up at the sky. "Megumi and the girls are lovely. He has a good job, a home, and his own child on the way."

Anna faced her mother. "But?"

"Oh, Anna. I didn't expect him to be so successful here. We had to support him for years, which your father was always reluctant to do. I had to be persistent, to give Rangi the benefit of the doubt. He struggled so much with drinking and trying to keep a job."

"He's made progress, Mum. Did you want him to be suffering here? For us to come and rescue him again?"

"I just didn't expect him to be doing so well without us."

"Well, we're here now. We get to see the life he's been living, to be with him again. I know it's been a journey, but we've all come a long way."

Isla began to cry. She lowered herself onto the doorstep.

"I feel like I'm lost, Anna. I'm so tired."

"It's been a long day, Mum." Anna sat next to her.

"I can't help thinking more and more about your experience going to Africa and then trying to adjust back to life here, and how Rangi didn't have the home with us he needed, either. I feel so guilty. I just want to do something to make it better, but instead I feel stuck."

"You're a saint, Mum. You've had to be the strongest one for so long. Life has moved so fast for you up until now." Anna scooted closer to her mother's spot on the step.

'I'm no saint. Saints take leaps of faith and accomplish mighty things. They make the world better. But our family has fallen apart on my watch. I've let things fester. I've been a coward."

'Come off it, Mum. I learned more about the good work of God's people by watching you raise us and serve our community than I did from all the missionaries I met in Kenya. You are a woman of love. It's in your bones. Our family may have scars, but we have the right stock. We're not lost."

Isla whimpered as she looked up at the stars, scanning across the sky above. The same stars that had watched over her father, and his before him. The same stars Yahweh told Abraham to count, as they were far fewer than his promised descendants.

'I could rattle off a thousand more excuses, but what you say is true." Isla closed her eyes and breathed deeply.

'You don't need more prodding from me. You just need to go in there and be with Rangi and his family. They're right here. Don't miss them now, Mum."

Behind them, the door screeched open and a pitter-patter of steps joined them on the stoop.

'Nana, would you come say goodnight?" said one voice.

'Please?" echoed the other.

'Is it Esther?" Isla turned and asked the shorter one, who stood just above her eye level.

The girl protested with a giggling contortion and quickly corrected Isla about her and her sister's names.

The light from the living room dimmed. Looming above Isla, Anna and the girls, Rangi stood in the doorway, his arm around Megumi's waist. His calm expression caused Isla's jaw to slacken and her heartbeat to still.

'You can even read them a story, like the ones you read to Anna and me," Rangi said, his gaze on her a silent conversation.

With her eyes, Isla thanked him. She sat, peaceful, on the threshold, a mother at her son's feet.

On Writing and Acknowledgment

Atlanta, USA, 2021

As I grow as a writer and a human being, I find increasingly that stories are a helpful processing tool, whether it be for personal reflection on upbringing and family history, current world events, or scenarios in the human experience that plunge the depths of emotion, meaning, pain and enlightenment. Endeavoring to write a story can be a harrowing and costly experience as much as it is rich and rewarding. It requires significant time and energy to render the complex nuance of our interior lives and how that overlays onto the exterior landscape around us (and vice versa). Self-doubt, ignorance, and fear of vulnerability are obstacles to writing narrative much in the same way as a lull in plot creativity. I wish to share some of the things I learned while writing this book.

More than a collection of words on a page, the texture and attitude of the story are the backdrop that add depth and realism for the reader. Thus, historical research, listening to and reading others' stories, and visiting real-world locations similar to a fictional setting are all tools I've sought to use in crafting these tales. In the end, I as the writer am shaped as much as the story.

This collection of short stories of a Waikato farming family started as a writing assignment: illustrate unresolved conflict in a scene of dialogue. I took that old writing maxim, "write what you know," and went to the fountain of family historical accounts. My dad's dad grew up as the youngest of seven on a farm in the verdant hills of New Zealand's Waikato region. Ever the storytellers, these siblings wrote and published a volume of family history later in their lives titled *Good Good - the Goodalls*.

There is a real concern that writing about family will be too "close to home," so I tried my best to use broad brushstrokes when painting this fictionalized portrait of my grandad's family. My goal was to have one foot in the past and one foot in the present, making sense of the generational impact of familial relationships while also rendering conversations and encounters I could be having in my life today. We are more than, but not less than, a collection of stories, our days filled with both heavy and lighthearted episodes that contribute to our personhood.

With the characters in the forefront of my mind, the format of the work quickly took shape. "The medium is the message," wrote Canadian philosopher Marshall McLuhan. I have found the literary form of a short story to be like an episode or snapshot, at times cozy and other times disturbing or prodding, but almost always a landing pad with enough space to observe a situation or idea in a meal-size package. In this way, illustrating family history and family member character studies lend themselves very well to a series of short stories.

Crafting the snapshots across this family history incorporated a number of recurring themes, the most impactful to me being reconciliation, acceptance and faith. As I fleshed out the backstories and motivations of each character in the family tree, I tried to communicate the tension I sensed existed between each of them: missed opportunities, disappointment, haunting memories of shame, misunderstood conversations, growing up and accepting the weight of responsibility, seeing your parents or children or siblings in a new light.

Experiencing life with family and our closest community shapes our worldview, can connect us with the divine, and instill in us values. It forms our sense of belonging and home. Unfortunately, those nearest to us can also inflict the deepest hurt, or even tiny, imperceptible offenses which snowball over time. Thankfully, we can also grow and mature and learn with each generation, while also holding on to the good and valuable things given to us by our ancestors. No matter how bleak the current state of a particular relationship, or even an entire family, I believe there is always hope for a step forward. It may take us out of our comfort zone to be known and understood, and it may look different than the home we started out in. We don't have to either reject or idolize the past, but if we can talk about and face it in our present, I believe that is where renewed belonging begins. That is what journeying with the Hester family taught me.

The pinnacle of this writing endeavor was the opportunity to inhabit the setting of these stories. My wife and I visited my family in New Zealand just before the onset of the Coronavirus pandemic in early 2020. It was a beautiful time, both magical and mundane, and helped me put the finishing touches on these stories—specifically, getting closer to the goal of conveying the uniqueness of Kiwi culture and the breathtaking landscapes of Aotearoa.

I want to thank those who have taught me about the craft of writing, including my writing teachers from grade school and Emory Continuing Education, as well as the Atlanta Writers Club. These stories were also inspired by the work of New Zealand authors Janet Frame and Barry Crump, as well as their American counterparts Flannery O'Conner, Toni Morrison, Mildred D. Taylor and John Steinbeck. Thank you to my editor, Elizabeth A. White, the cover artist Elizabeth Lang, and my friends who proofread the book.

Lastly, thank you to my parents, grandparents, brothers, and cousins across the world, and most especially to my wife, Becca. Thank you for "loving me into being" as Fred Rogers said. Thank you for being my community. Here's to the great stories, messy stories, and redemptive stories that have been and will be told in our lives. I'm glad to live them out inspired by and together with you.

About the Author

Joseph R. Goodall was born in Auckland, New Zealand and spent his childhood in Florida. Inspired by books combining science, history and creative story-telling, he wrote and illustrated his own stories from an early age. A big backyard, close-knit extended family, and involvement in community service efforts all shaped his love of building relationships and exploring cities, parks and nature trails. Humanitarian aid efforts have taken him on trips to Bolivia, India and Haiti, deepening his curiosity about the significance of place-making, the way people live, and how to develop cross-cultural partnerships.

A licensed engineer with a degree from the University of Florida, he has worked in land development for over five years, preparing site designs for housing communities, office developments, parks and a wastewater treatment plant.

His writing focuses on family, faith, community relationships, identity, and coming-of-age. He is working on his first novel.

Joseph and his wife, Becca, live in Atlanta, GA.

For more information and updates, visit: www.jrgoodall.com.